Homer Price

Written and illustrated

By ROBERT McCLOSKEY

SCHOLASTIC INC.
New York Toronto London Auckland Sydney

Also by Robert McCloskey:

Lentil

Make Way for Ducklings

Centerburg Tales

Blueberries for Sal

One Morning in Maine

Time of Wonder

ISBN 0-590-09049-6

72 71 70 69 68 67 66 65 64 63 62   7 8 9/0

Printed in the U.S.A.   40

CONTENTS

I

The Case of the Sensational Scent

The Case of the
Sensational Scent

ABOUT two miles outside of Centerburg, where route 56 meets route 56A, there lives a boy named Homer. Homer's father owns a tourist camp. Homer's mother cooks fried chicken and hamburgers in the lunchroom and takes care of the tourist cabins while his father takes care of the filling station. Homer does odd jobs about the place. Sometimes he washes windshields of cars to help his father, and sometimes he sweeps out cabins or takes care of the lunchroom to help his mother.

When Homer isn't going to school, or doing odd jobs, or playing with other boys, he works on his hobby, which is building radios. He has a workshop in one corner of his room, where he works in the evenings.

Before going to bed at night he usually goes down

to the kitchen to have a glass of milk and cookies because working on radios makes him hungry. Tabby, the family cat, usually comes around for something to eat too.

One night Homer came down and opened the ice-box door, and poured a saucer of milk for Tabby and a glass of milk for himself. He put the bottle back and looked to see if there was anything interesting on the other shelves. He heard footsteps and felt something soft brush his leg, so he reached down to pet Tabby. When he looked down, the animal drinking the milk certainly wasn't a cat! It was a skunk! Homer was startled just a little but he didn't make any sudden motions, because he remembered what he had read about skunks. They can make a very strong smell that people and other animals don't like. But the smell is only for protection, and if you don't frighten them, or hurt them, they are very friendly.

While the skunk finished drinking the saucer of milk, Homer decided to keep it for a pet, because he had read somewhere that skunks become excellent pets if you treat them kindly. He decided to name the skunk "Aroma." Then he poured out some more milk for Aroma, and had some more himself. Aroma finished the second saucer of milk, licked his mouth, and calmly started to walk away. Homer followed and found that Aroma's home was under the house right beneath his window.

During the next few days Homer did a lot of thinking about what would be the best way to tame Aroma. He didn't know what his mother would think of a pet skunk around the house, but he said to himself Aroma has been living under the house all this time and nobody knew about it, so I guess it will be all right for it to keep on being a secret.

He took a saucer of milk out to Aroma every evening when nobody was looking and in a few weeks Aroma was just as tame as a puppy.

Homer thought it would be nice if he could bring Aroma up to his room because it would be good to have company while he worked building radios. So he got an old basket and tied a rope to the handle to make an elevator. He let the basket down from his window and trained Aroma to climb in when he gave a low whistle. Then he would pull the rope and up came the basket, and up came Aroma to pay a social call. Aroma spent most of his visit sleeping, while Homer worked on a new radio. Aroma's favorite place to sleep was in Homer's suitcase.

One evening Homer said, "There, that's the last

wire soldered and my new radio is finished. I'll put the new tubes in it, then we can try it out!" Aroma opened one eye and didn't look interested, even when the radio worked perfectly and an announcer's voice said, "N. W. Blott of Centerburg won the grand prize of two thousand dollars for writing the best slogan about Dreggs After-Shaving Lotion."

"Why I know him, and he's from my town!" said Homer.

Aroma still looked uninterested while the announcer said that next week they would broadcast the Dreggs program from Centerburg and that Mr. Dreggs himself would give Mr. N. W. Blott the two thousand dollars cash and one dozen bottles of Dreggs Lotion for thinking up the best advertising slogan. "Just think, Aroma, a real radio broadcast from Centerburg! I'll have to see that!"

The day of the broadcast arrived and Homer rode to Centerburg on his bicycle to watch. He was there early and he got a good place right next to the man who worked the controls so he could see everything that happened.

Mr. Dreggs made a speech about the wonderful thing Mr. N. W. Blott had contributed to the future of American shaving with his winning slogan: "The after-shave lotion with the distinctive invigorating

smell that keeps you on your toes." Then he gave
N. W. the two thousand and one dozen bottles of
lotion in a suitcase just like the one that Homer had
at home. After N. W. made a short speech the program was over. Just then four men said, "Put 'em up,"
and then one of them said to N. W., "If you please,"
and grabbed the suitcase with all of the money and

lotion inside it. Everyone was surprised — Mr. Dreggs was surprised, N. W. Blott was surprised, the announcer was surprised, the radio control man was surprised — and everybody was frightened too. The robbers were gone before anybody knew what happened. They jumped into a car and were out of sight down route 56A before the sheriff shouted,

"Wait till I send out an alarm, men, then we'll chase them. No robio raiders, I mean radio robbers, can do that in this town and get away again!" The sheriff sent out an alarm to the State Police, and then some of the men took their shotguns and went off down 56A in the sheriff's car.

Homer waited around until the sheriff and the men came back and the sheriff said, "They got clean away. There's not hide or hare of 'em the whole length of 56 or 56A."

While they were eating dinner that evening, Homer told the family about what had happened in town. After helping with the dishes he went up to his room, and after he had pulled Aroma up in the basket he listened to the news report of the robbery on his new radio. "The police are baffled," the news commentator said, "Mr. N. W. Blott is offering half of the prize money and six bottles of the lotion to anyone who helps him get his prize back."

"Aroma, if we could just catch those robbers we would have enough money to build lots of radios and even a television receiver!" said Homer.

He decided that he had better go to bed instead of trying to think of a way to catch robbers, because he was going to get up very early the next morning and go fishing.

He woke up before it was light, slipped on his pants, and ate a bowl of cereal. Then he found his fishing pole and gave a low whistle for Aroma (the whistle wasn't necessary because Aroma was waiting in the basket). Homer put the basket on his bike and they rode off down 56A.

They turned into the woods where the bridge crossed the brook. And Homer parked the bike and started to walk along the brook with Aroma following right along.

They fished all morning but didn't catch anything because the fish just weren't biting. They tried all of the best places in the brook, and when they were ready to go home they decided to go straight through the woods instead of following the brook because the woods path was much shorter.

The path through the woods was an old wood road that was not used any more. It had not been used for years and almost everybody had forgotten that it was ever built. Before they had gone very far Homer thought he heard voices, then he smelled bacon cooking. He thought it was strange because nobody ever came up on this mountain to camp, so he decided to sneak up and investigate.

When Homer and Aroma looked around a large rock they saw four men! "THE ROBBERS!" whispered Homer, and indeed they were the robbers.

There was the suitcase with the two thousand dollars and the one dozen bottles of after-shaving lotion lying open on the ground. The robbers had evidently just gotten up because they were cooking breakfast over an open fire and their faces were covered with soapy lather, for they were shaving.

Homer was so interested in what the robbers were doing that he forgot to keep an eye on Aroma. The next thing he knew, Aroma had left the hiding place and was walking straight toward the suitcase! He climbed inside and curled up on the packages of money and went right to sleep. The robbers were busy shaving, and having a difficult time of it too, because they had only one little mirror and they were all stooped over trying to look in it.

"I can hardly wait to finish shaving and try some of that fragrant after-shaving lotion," said the first robber.

Then the second robber (who had a cramp in his back from stooping over and from sleeping in the woods) straightened up and turned around. He noticed Aroma and said, "Look at that thing in our money!" The other robbers turned around and looked surprised.

"That, my dear friend, is *not* a thing. It is a Musteline Mammal *(Genus Mephitis)* commonly known as a *skunk!*" said the third robber, who had evidently gone to college and studied zoology.

"Well I don't care if it's a thing or a mammal or a skunk, he can't sleep on our money. I'll cook that mammal's goose!" Then he picked up a big gun and pointed it at Aroma.

"I wouldn't do that if I were you," said the third robber with the college education. "It might attract the sheriff, and besides it isn't the accepted thing to do to Musteline Mammals."

So the robbers put a piece of bacon on the end of a stick and tried to coax Aroma out of the suitcase, but Aroma just sniffed at the bacon, yawned, and went back to sleep.

Now the fourth robber picked up a rock and said, "This will scare it away!" The rock went sailing through the aid and landed with an alarming crash! It missed Aroma, but it broke a half dozen bottles of Mr. Dreggs' lotion. The air was filled with "that distinctive invigorating smell that keeps you on your toes," but mostly, the air was filled with Aroma!

Everybody ran, because the smell was so strong it made you want to close your eyes.

Homer waited by the old oak tree for Aroma to catch up, but not for Aroma to catch up all the way.

They came to the bike and rode off at full speed.

Except to stop once to put Aroma and the basket on the rear mudguard, they made the trip home in record time.

Homer was very thoughtful while he did the odd jobs that afternoon. He thought he had better tell his mother what had happened up on the mountain. (His father had gone into the city to buy some things that were needed around the place, and he would not be back until late that night.) At dinnertime he was just about to tell her when she said, "I think I smell a skunk around here. I'll tell your father when he gets home. We will have to get rid of that animal right away because people will not want to spend the night at our tourist camp if we have that smell around." Then Homer decided not to say anything about it, because he didn't want his father to get rid of Aroma, and because the robbers would no doubt get caught by the State police anyway.

That evening Homer was taking care of the gas station and helping his mother while his father was in the city. In between cooking hamburgers and putting gas in cars, he read the radio builders' magazine and looked at the pictures in the mail-order catalogue. About eight o'clock four men got out of a car and said, "We would like to rent a tourist cabin for the night."

Homer said, "All right, follow me," and he led the way to one of the largest cabins.

"I think you will be comfortable here," he said, "and that will be four dollars in advance, please."

"Here's a five-dollar bill, Buddy, you can keep the change," said one of the men.

"Thanks," said Homer as he stuffed the bill in his pocket and hurried out the door because there was a car outside honking for gas.

He was just about to put the five-dollar bill in the cash register when he smelled that strange mixture, partly "the distinctive invigorating smell that keeps you on your toes" and partly Aroma. He sniffed the bill and sure enough, that was what he had smelled!

"The robbers! Those four men are the robbers!" said Homer to himself.

He decided that he had better call up the sheriff and tell him everything. He knew that the sheriff would be down at the barbershop in Centerburg playing checkers and talking politics with his friends, this being Saturday night. He waited until his mother was busy getting an extra blanket for someone because he did not think it was necessary to frighten her. Then he called the barbershop and asked to talk to the sheriff.

"Hello," said Homer to the sheriff, "those four robbers are spending the night out here at our tourist camp. Why don't you come out and arrest them?"

"Well, I'll be switched," said the sheriff. "Have they got the money and the lotion with them?"

"Yes, they brought it," said Homer.

"Well, have they got their guns along too?" asked the sheriff.

"I don't know, but if you hold the line a minute I'll slip out and look," said Homer.

He slipped out and peeped through the window of the robbers' cabin. They were getting undressed, and their guns were lying on the table and on the chairs and under the bed and on the dresser — there were lots of guns. Homer slipped back and told the sheriff, "They must have a dozen or two."

The sheriff said, "They have, huh? Well, I tell you, sonny, I'm just about to get my hair cut, so you jest sorta keep your eye on 'em and I'll be out there in about an hour or so. That'll give them time to get to sleep; then some of the boys and me can walk right in and snap the bracelets on 'em."

"O.K. See you later, Sheriff," said Homer.

Later when his mother came in, Homer said, "Mother, I have some very important business, do you think that you could take care of things for a while?"

"Well, I think so, Homer," said his mother, "but don't stay away too long."

Homer slipped up to a window in the robbers' cabin and started keeping an eye on them.

They were just getting into bed, and they were not in a very good humor because they had been arguing about how to divide the money and the six bottles of lotion that were left.

They were afraid, too, that one of the four might get up in the night and run away with the suitcase, with the money and the lotion in it. They finally decided to sleep all four in one bed, because if one of them got out of bed it would surely wake the others. It was a tight fit, but they all managed to get into bed and get themselves covered up. They put the suitcase with the money and the lotion inside right in the middle of the bed. After they had turned out the light, it was very quiet for a long while, then the first robber said, "You know, this ain't so comfortable, sleeping four in a bed."

"I know," the second robber said, "but it's better than sleeping in the woods where there are mosquitoes."

"And funny little animals that don't smell so nice," added the third robber.

"You must admit, though, that our present condition could be described as being a trifle overcrowded," said the one with the college education.

"Them's my feelings exactly," said the first robber. "We might as well start driving to Mexico, because we can't sleep like this. We might as well ride toward the border."

"No, driving at night makes me nervous," said the second robber.

"Me too," said the third. Then there followed a long argument, with the first and third robbers trying to convince the second and fourth robbers that they should go to Mexico right away. While they were arguing Homer thought very hard. He guessed that something had better be done pretty quick, or the robbers might decide to go before the sheriff got his hair cut. He thought of a plan, and without making a sound, he slipped away from the window and hurried to Aroma's hole under the house. He whistled softly and Aroma came out and climbed into the basket. Aroma had calmed down considerably, but she still smelled pretty strong. Homer quietly carried the basket to the spot under the robbers' window and listened. They were still arguing about the trip to Mexico. They didn't notice Homer as he put the basket through the window onto the chair beside the bed. Of course, Aroma immediately crawled out on the bed and took her place on the suitcase.

"Stop tickling," said the tall robber because his feet stuck out and Aroma's tail was resting on his toes.

"I'm not tickling you," said the second robber, "but say, I think I still smell that animal!"

"Now that you mention it, I seem to smell it too," said the third robber.

The fourth robber reached for the light button saying, "That settles it! Let's get dressed and go to Mexico, because *I think I smell that animal too!*"

Then as the robber turned on the light Homer shouted, "You *do* smell that animal, and please don't make any sudden movements because he excites easily." The robbers took one look and pulled the covers over their heads.

"The sheriff will be here in a few minutes," said Homer bravely.

But five minutes later the sheriff had not shown up. The robbers were getting restless, and Aroma was tapping her foot and getting excited.

Homer began to be disturbed about what his mother would say if Aroma smelled up one of her largest and best tourist cabins, so he quickly thought of a plan. He climbed through the window. He gathered up all of the guns and put them in the basket.

Then he gathered up the robbers' clothes and tossed them out of the window. After picking out one of the larger guns Homer waved it in the direction of the robbers and said, "You may come out from under the covers now, and hold up your hands."

The robbers gingerly lifted the covers and peeked out, then they carefully climbed out of bed so as not to disturb Aroma, and put up their hands.

"We didn't *mean* to do it," mumbled the first robber.

"And we'll give the money back," said the second robber.

"Our early environment is responsible for our actions," said the educated robber.

"I'm sorry," Homer said, "but I'll have to take you to the sheriff." He motioned with the gun and demanded that the fourth robber pick up the suitcase with the prize money and lotion inside. Then he said, "Forward march!"

"Must we go in our pajamas?" cried one.

"And without our shoes?" wailed another.

"Aroma is getting excited," Homer reminded them, and the robbers started marching without any more arguing, but they did grumble and groan about walking on gravel with bare feet (robbers aren't accustomed to going without shoes, and they couldn't have run away, even if Homer and Aroma hadn't been there to guard them).

First came the first robber with his hands up, then the second robber with his hands up, then the third robber with his hands up, and then the fourth robber with his right hand up and his left hand down, carrying the suitcase (of course Aroma followed the suitcase), and last of all came Homer, carrying the basket with a dozen or two guns in it. He marched them straight down route 56A and up the main street of Centerburg. They turned into the barbershop where the sheriff was getting his hair cut and the boys were sitting around playing checkers.

When the sheriff saw them come in the door he stopped talking about the World Series and said, "Well, I'll be switched, if it ain't the robio raiders, I mean radio robbers!" The sheriff got out of the barber chair with his hair cut up one side and not cut up the other and put handcuffs on the men and led them off to the jail.

Well, there isn't much more to tell. The newspapers told the story and had headlines saying, BOY AND PET SKUNK TRAP SHAVING LOTION ROBBERS BY SMELL, and the news commentators on the radio told about it too. Homer's father and mother said

that Homer could keep Aroma for a pet because instead of hurting business Aroma has doubled business. People for miles around are coming to the crossroads where 56 meets 56A just to buy gasoline and to eat a hamburger or a home-cooked dinner, and to see Aroma.

The next time Homer went into Centerburg to get a haircut he talked the whole thing over again with the sheriff.

"Yep!" said the sheriff, "that was sure one smell job of swelling, I mean one swell job of smelling!"

2

The Case of the Cosmic Comic

The Case of the
Cosmic Comic

ONE Saturday afternoon Homer and Freddy and Freddy's little brother Louis were listening to the State College football game on the radio.

After the game Homer said, "I'm feeling sort of hungry. Come on, Freddy, come on, Louis. Let's go down to the kitchen and get something to eat."

They went downstairs and Homer poured out three glasses of milk, and Homer's mother brought out the cookie jar.

"Don't eat too many cookies," she cautioned, "because it's almost dinnertime."

"No, Ma'm, we won't," said Freddy. Then he said to Homer, "Has tonight's newspaper come yet?"

"I think so," said Homer. "Yes, there it is, on top of the refrigerator."

"Oh, boy!" said Freddy as he opened it to the comic page. "Let's see what happened to the 'Super-Duper.'"

So Freddy and little brother Louis and Homer gathered around the paper to see how the Super-Duper was going to get out of the big steel box filled with dynamite, where the villain had put him and dropped him into the middle of the ocean from an airship.

There in the first picture, the Super-Duper was saying, "Haw, Haw! That villain thinks he can get rid of me, but he's mistaken!" Then in the next picture the dynamite exploded and blew the steel box to bits. But that didn't hurt the Super-Duper because the Super-Duper is *so* tough (tougher than steel) that *nothing* can hurt *him!*

"Just look at those muscles and that chest the Super-Duper's got!" said Freddy before going on to the next picture. In the next picture the Super-Duper bounded up from the bottom of the ocean and went whizzing through the air. He caught the airship by the tail and broke it off with a loud *crack!* In the last picture the villain was trying to escape in an airplane, and was machine-gunning the Super-Duper, but the bullets were just bouncing off his chest because he was so tough. Then it said, "Continued on Monday."

"Boy!" said Freddy, "the Super-Duper can do anything!"

"Yeh, but it's only a story," said Homer. "And the story's always the same. The Super-Duper always hits things and breaks them up, and a villain always tries to bomb him, or shoot him with a cannon or a gun or an electric ray. Then he always rescues the pretty girl and gets the villain in the end."

"Well, it isn't just a story," said Freddy, "because Super-Duper's in the movies too. They really take *movies* of him lifting battleships with one hand and even flying through space."

"Aw," said Homer, "I read a book once that said they do that sort of thing with wires and mirrors. It's just trick photography, that's all it is."

Then little brother Louis, who had been eating cookies all this time said, "Read it to me!"

So Freddy had to read it all over again, out loud, and explain the story to little Louis.

"Freddy," called Homer's mother, "your mother just phoned and wants you to bring little Louis right home."

"O.K. C'mon, Louis, finish your milk. Good-by, Homer, and thank you for the cookies."

The next time Freddy came over to visit Homer he brought along some of his Super-Duper comic magazines.

"Say, Homer, I thought you might like to look at these," said Freddy.

"Gosh, Freddy, you certainly have a lot of those comic magazines," said Homer.

"They don't cost much," said Freddy. "Only ten cents apiece. Here, read this one, Homer, it's the most exciting."

Homer took the comic magazine and started to read, while Freddy looked over his shoulder.

At the beginning of the story the Super-Duper was

dressed in ordinary clothes, just like any other man. Then after the villain appeared on the second page, the Super-Duper slipped behind a tree and changed into red tights and a long blue cape.

"Why does he always change his clothes like that?" asked Homer.

"That's because he is so modest," said Freddy in a knowing way. Homer started reading again: After the Super-Duper had changed his clothes he started flying through space and smashing things. He picked up automobiles and tossed them over cliffs, and he even carried a train across a river after the villain had blown up the bridge.

Then finally he saved the pretty girl from a horrible death and caught the villain, who turned out to be a very notorious criminal.

"Gosh, Freddy, these Super-Duper stories are all the same," said Homer.

"No, they're not!" said Freddy. "Sometimes the Super-Duper smashes airships and sometimes he smashes ocean liners. Then, other times he just breaks up mountains."

"But he always rescues the pretty girl and catches the villain on the last page," said Homer.

"Of course," said Freddy. "That's to show that crime does not pay!"

"Shucks!" said Homer. "Let's go pitch horseshoes."

"O.K.," said Freddy.

Freddy won two games out of three and then he said, "Guess it's almost suppertime, see you tomorrow, Homer."

"Yep! G'by, Freddy," said Homer, and Freddy gathered up his comic magazines and went up the road home.

After supper, when Homer was doing his homework, the phone rang. "Hello!" said Homer.

"Hello, that you, Homer? This is Freddy. Say! Did you see in the paper tonight that there is going to be a Super-Duper movie over at the Centerburg theater next Saturday afternoon?"

Before Homer could say, "No, I didn't." Freddy shouted, "And guess what! The Super-Duper in person is going to be there! And, Homer," Freddy went on, "Mother has a box from the mail-order house over at the Centerburg Railroad station. So Dad says that little Louis and I can take the horse and wagon and drive to Centerburg on Saturday. We can get the box and then go to see the Super-Duper! I thought you might like to come along."

"Sure thing!" said Homer.

"O.K. We'll stop by for you," said Freddy. "G'by, Homer."

On Saturday Freddy and little Louis drove up to Homer's house, with old Lucy hitched to the wagon, just as Homer was finishing his lunch.

"I thought we had better get an early start," said Freddy, "because it takes old Lucy about an hour to go as far as Centerburg."

"I'll be ready in just a second," said Homer. Then after Homer had climbed in, Freddy said "Giddap!" to old Lucy, and they started off to see the Super-Duper in person.

When they arrived in Centerburg the first thing they did was go to the station and load the box from the mail-order house onto the back of the wagon.

"Gosh, that's heavy!" said Homer as they lifted it on.

"Yeah," said Freddy, "but I betcha the Super-Duper could lift it with his little finger."

"Mebby so," said Homer. "Let's stop over at Uncle Ulysses' lunchroom and get some doughnuts to eat in the movies."

Freddy and little Louis both thought that was a good idea, so they drove old Lucy around to the lunchroom to get some doughnuts.

Then Freddy and little Louis and Homer walked across the town square to the movie.

The Super-Duper's super-stream-lined car was

standing in front of the theater. It was long and red, with chromium trimmings, and it had the Super-Duper's monogram on the side. After they had admired the car, they bought three tickets and went inside.

There in the lobby was the *real honest-to-goodness* Super-Duper. He shook hands with Freddy and Homer and little brother Louis, and he autographed a card for Freddy, too.

"Mr. Super-Duper, would you please do a little flying through space for us, or mebbe just bend a few horseshoes?" asked Freddy.

"I'm sorry, boys, but I haven't time today," said the Super-Duper with a smile.

So Homer and Freddy and little Louis found three good seats and ate doughnuts until the picture began.

The picture was called "THE SUPER-DUPER and the ELECTRIC RAY." That was because the villain had a machine that produced an electric ray, and every time he shined it on a skyscraper, or an airplane, the skyscraper or the airplane would explode! He turned the ray on Super-Duper, too, but of course the Super-Duper was so tough that it didn't hurt *him.*

Little Louis got so excited, though, that he choked on a doughnut and Homer had to take him to the lobby for a drink of water. But finally the Super-Duper broke the villain's headquarters to bits, and lifted the ray machine (which must have weighed several tons) and tossed it over a cliff. *Then* he caught the villain and rescued the pretty girl. But at the very end, the villain slipped away again, and then these words appeared on the screen: "NEXT IN-STALLMENT NEXT SATURDAY AFTERNOON!"

"Why did the Super-Duper let the villain get away again?" asked little Louis on the way out.

"I guess that's because he wants to chase him again next Saturday," said Homer.

Outside they admired the Super-Duper's car once more and then started home in the wagon.

It was evening by the time old Lucy, pulling the wagon with Freddy and little Louis and Homer on it, had reached the curve in the road just before you come to Homer's father's filling station.

A car honked from behind and Freddy pulled old Lucy over to the edge of the road. Then, "SWOOSH!" around from the rear sped a long red car with chrom-ium trimmings.

"Gosh! It's the Super-Duper!" said Freddy.

"Well, he shouldn't drive so fast around this curve," said Homer, sort of doubtful like.

Almost before Homer had finished speaking there was a loud screech of brakes, and then a loud crash!

"Giddup! Lucy," said Freddy, "we better hurry up and see what happened!"

"Gee, there weren't any cars coming the other way," said Homer, "I wonder what happened?"

"Golly," said Freddy in a quavery voice, "do you suppose . . . the electric ray? . . . Whoow, Lucy, WHOO, LUCY! . . . we better park here!"

"Oh, shucks!" said Homer in his bravest voice, "I'm going to see what happened."

Little Louis began to cry, and Homer tried to comfort him. "Louis, that electric ray business was just part of a movie, and it couldn't have anything to do with this." Homer tried hard to make it sound convincing.

Then Homer and Freddy and little Louis got out of the wagon and crept along the side of the road.

There, around the curve, was the Super-Duper's car, down in a ditch. All three boys stopped crawling along and lay down on their stomachs to watch.

"Oh, boy!" whispered Freddy. "Now we'll get to see the Super-Duper lift it back on the road with one hand!"

There was a flash of light and little Louis cried, "Is that the electric ray?"

"It's only the headlights of a car," said Homer. "Come on, let's go a little closer."

They crept a little closer... They could see the Super-Duper now, sitting there in the twilight with his head in his hands.

"I wonder if he got hurt?" asked Homer.

"Naaw!" whispered Freddy. "Nothing can hurt the Super-Duper because he's too tough."

"Well, if he isn't hurt, why doesn't he lift the car back on the road?" asked Homer.

"Sh-h-h!" said Freddy, "he's an awful modest fellow." So they waited and watched from the bushes.

The Super-Duper sighed a couple of times, and then he got up and started walking around his car.

"Now watch!" said Freddy in a loud whisper. "Oh, boy! Oh, boy!" The Super-Duper didn't lift the car, no, not yet. He looked at the dent that a fence post had made in his shiny red fender, and *then*, the incredible happened. That colossal-osal, gigantic-antic Super-Duper, that same Super-Duper who defied the elements, who was so strong that he broke up battleships like toothpicks, who was so tough that cannon balls bounced off his chest, yes, who was *tougher* than steel, he stooped down and said . . . "Ouch!" Yes, there could be no mistake, he said it again, louder . . . "OUCH ! !"

The great Super-Duper had gotten himself caught on a barbed-wire fence!

"Well . . . well, for crying out loud!" said Freddy.

"What happened?" asked little Louis. "Did he get himself rayed by the villain?"

"Come on, Freddy, let's go and untangle him," said Homer. Then Freddy and little Louis and Homer unsnagged the Super-Duper and he sighed again and said, "Thank you boys. Do you know if there's a garage near here? It looks as though it will take a wrecking car to get my car out of this ditch."

"Sure, my father has a garage down at the crossing," said Homer. "And we have a horse right up there on the road. We can pull your car out of the ditch!" said Freddy.

"Well, now, isn't that lucky!" said Super-Duper with a smile.

So they hitched old Lucy to the car, and she pulled and everybody pushed until the car was back on the road.

Little Louis sat with the Super-Duper in his car, and Homer and Freddy rode on old Lucy's back while she towed the car toward Homer's father's filling station.

"What happened, Mr. Super-Duper, did the villain ray you?" asked little Louis.

"No," said the Super-Duper, and he laughed. "When I drove around that curve, there was a skunk right in the middle of the road. I didn't want to hit him and get this new car all smelled up, so, I went into the ditch. Ha! Ha!"

When they had reached the filling station, they put some iodine on the scratches that the barbed wire had made on the Super-Duper. (He made faces, just like anybody else, when it was daubed on.) Then he ate a hamburger, and by that time Homer's father had the car fixed, except for the dent in the fender. Before the Super-Duper drove away, he thanked the boys and made them a present of a large stack of Super-Duper comic books. After he'd gone, Homer and Freddy went back with old Lucy to get the wagon.

"Well, anyway, Freddy, we've got a complete set of Super-Duper comic books," said Homer.

"Yeah," said Freddy. Then he said, "Say, Homer, do me a favor, will you, and don't tell anybody about the Super-Duper and the barbed wire and the ditch and the iodine, especially Artie Bush. If he doesn't hear about this I might be able to trade my comic books for that baseball bat of his, the Louisville Slugger that's only slightly cracked."

"O.K." said Homer. "Come to think of it, his cousin, Skinny, has a pretty good ball, too. This is a good time to get even for the time Skinny traded me a bicycle bell that wouldn't ring for my nearly new bugle."

3

The Doughnuts

The Doughnuts

ONE Friday night in November Homer overheard his mother talking on the telephone to Aunt Agnes over in Centerburg. "I'll stop by with the car in about half an hour and we can go to the meeting together," she said, because tonight was the night the Ladies' Club was meeting to discuss plans for a box social and to knit and sew for the Red Cross.

"I think I'll come along and keep Uncle Ulysses company while you and Aunt Agnes are at the meeting," said Homer.

So after Homer had combed his hair and his mother had looked to see if she had her knitting instructions and the right size needles, they started for town.

Homer's Uncle Ulysses and Aunt Agnes have a very up-and-coming lunchroom over in Centerburg, just across from the court house on the town square. Uncle Ulysses is a man with advanced ideas and a weakness for labor-saving devices. He equipped the lunchroom with automatic toasters, automatic coffee maker, automatic dishwasher, and an automatic doughnut maker. All just the latest thing in labor-saving devices. Aunt Agnes would throw up her hands and sigh every time Uncle Ulysses bought a new labor-saving device. Sometimes she became unkindly disposed toward him for days and days. She was of the opinion that Uncle Ulysses just frittered away his spare time over at the barbershop with the sheriff and the boys, so, what was the good of a labor-saving device that gave you more time to fritter?

When Homer and his mother got to Centerburg, they stopped at the lunchroom, and after Aunt Agnes had come out and said, "My, how that boy does grow!" which was what she always said, she went off with Homer's mother in the car. Homer went into the lunchroom and said, "Howdy, Uncle Ulysses!"

"Oh, hello, Homer. You're just in time," said Uncle Ulysses. "I've been going over this automatic doughnut machine, oiling the machinery and cleaning the works . . . wonderful things, these labor-saving devices."

"Yep," agreed Homer, and he picked up a cloth

and started polishing the metal trimmings while Uncle Ulysses tinkered with the inside workings.

"Opfwo-oof! !" sighed Uncle Ulysses and, "Look here, Homer, you've got a mechanical mind. See if you can find where these two pieces fit in. I'm going across to the barbershop for a spell, 'cause there's somethin' I've got to talk to the sheriff about. There won't be much business here until the double feature is over and I'll be back before then."

Then as Uncle Ulysses went out the door he said, "Uh, Homer, after you get the pieces in place, would you mind mixing up a batch of doughnut batter and putting it in the machine? You could turn the switch and make a few doughnuts to have on hand for the crowd after the movie . . . if you don't mind."

"O.K." said Homer, "I'll take care of everything."

A few minutes later a customer came in and said, "Good evening, Bud."

Homer looked up from putting the last piece in the doughnut machine and said, "Good evening, Sir, what can I do for you?"

"Well, young feller, I'd like a cup o' coffee and some doughnuts," said the customer.

"I'm sorry, Mister, but we won't have any dough-nuts for about half an hour, until I can mix some dough and start this machine. I could give you some very fine sugar rolls instead."

"Well, Bud, I'm in no real hurry so I'll just have a cup o' coffee and wait around a bit for the doughnuts. Fresh doughnuts are always worth waiting for is what I always say."

"O.K.," said Homer, and he drew a cup of coffee from Uncle Ulysses' superautomatic coffee maker.

"Nice place you've got here," said the customer.

"Oh, yes," replied Homer, "this is a very up-and-coming lunchroom with all the latest improvements."

"Yes," said the stranger, "must be a good business. I'm in business too. A traveling man in outdoor advertising. I'm a sandwich man. Mr. Gabby's my name."

"My name is Homer. I'm glad to meet you, Mr. Gabby. It must be a fine profession, traveling and advertising sandwiches."

"Oh no," said Mr. Gabby, "I don't advertise sandwiches. I just wear any kind of an ad, one sign on front and one sign on behind, this way . . . Like a sandwich. Ya know what I mean?"

"Oh, I see. That must be fun, and you travel too?" asked Homer as he got out the flour and the baking powder.

"Yeah, I ride the rods between jobs, on freight trains, ya know what I mean?"

"Yes, but isn't that dangerous?" asked Homer.

"Of course there's a certain amount a risk, but you take any method a travel these days it's all dangerous. Ya know what I mean? Now take airplanes for instance . . ."

Just then a large shiny black car stopped in front of the lunchroom and a chauffeur helped a lady out of the rear door. They both came inside and the lady smiled at Homer and said, "We've stopped for a light snack. Some doughnuts and coffee would be simply marvelous."

Then Homer said, "I'm sorry, Ma'm, but the doughnuts won't be ready until I make this batter and start Uncle Ulysses' doughnut machine."

"Well now aren't *you* a clever young man to know how to make *doughnuts!*"

"Well," blushed Homer, "I've really never done it before, but I've got a recipe to follow."

"Now, young man, you simply must allow me to help. You know, I haven't made doughnuts for years, but I know the best recipe for doughnuts. It's marvelous, and we really must use it."

"But, Ma'm . . ." said Homer.

"Now just *wait* till you taste these doughnuts," said the lady. "Do you have an apron?" she asked, as she took off her fur coat and her rings and her jewelry and rolled up her sleeves. "Charles," she said to the

chauffeur, "hand me that baking powder, that's right, and, young man, we'll need some nutmeg."

So Homer and the chauffeur stood by and handed things and cracked the eggs while the lady mixed and stirred. Mr. Gabby sat on his stool, sipped his coffee, and looked on with great interest.

"There!" said the lady when all of the ingredients were mixed. "Just *wait* till you taste these doughnuts!"

"It looks like an awful lot of batter," said Homer as he stood on a chair and poured it into the doughnut machine with the help of the chauffeur. "It's about *ten* times as much as Uncle Ulysses ever makes."

"But wait till you taste them!" said the lady with an eager look and a smile.

Homer got down from the chair and pushed a button on the machine marked, *Start*. Rings of batter started dropping into the hot fat. After a ring of batter was cooked on one side, an automatic gadget turned it over and the other side would cook. Then another automatic gadget gave the doughnut a little push and it rolled neatly down a little chute, all ready to eat.

"That's a simply *fascinating* machine," said the lady as she waited for the first doughnut to roll out.

"Here, young man, *you* must have the first one. Now isn't that just *too* delicious!? Isn't it simply marvelous?"

"Yes, Ma'm, it's very good," replied Homer as the lady handed doughnuts to Charles and to Mr. Gabby, and asked if they didn't think they were simply divine doughnuts.

"It's an old family recipe!" said the lady with pride.

Homer poured some coffee for the lady and her chauffeur and for Mr. Gabby, and a glass of milk for himself. Then they all sat down at the lunch counter to enjoy another few doughnuts apiece.

"I'm so glad you enjoy my doughnuts," said the lady. "But now, Charles, we really must be going. If you will just take this apron, Homer, and put two dozen doughnuts in a bag to take along, we'll be on our way. And, Charles, don't forget to pay the young man." She rolled down her sleeves and put on her jewelry; then Charles managed to get her into her big fur coat.

"Good night, young man, I haven't had so much fun in years. I *really* haven't!" said the lady, as she went out the door and into the big shiny car.

"Those are sure good doughnuts," said Mr. Gabby as the car moved off.

"You bet!" said Homer. Then he and Mr. Gabby

stood and watched the automatic doughnut machine make doughnuts.

After a few dozen more doughnuts had rolled down the little chute, Homer said, "I guess that's about enough doughnuts to sell to the aftertheater customers. I'd better turn the machine off for a while."

Homer pushed the button marked *Stop* and there was a little click, but nothing happened. The rings of batter kept right on dropping into the hot fat, and an automatic gadget kept right on turning them over, and another automatic gadget kept right on giving them a little push, and the doughnuts kept right on rolling down the little chute, all ready to eat.

"That's funny," said Homer, "I'm sure that's the right button!" He pushed it again but the automatic doughnut maker kept right on making doughnuts.

"Well I guess I must have put one of those pieces in backwards," said Homer.

"Then it might stop if you pushed the button marked *Start*," said Mr. Gabby.

Homer did, and the doughnuts still kept rolling down the little chute, just as regular as a clock can tick.

"I guess we could sell a few more doughnuts," said Homer, "but I'd better telephone Uncle Ulysses over at the barbershop." Homer gave the number, and while he waited for someone to answer he counted thirty-seven doughnuts roll down the little chute.

Finally someone answered "Hello! This is the sarberbhop, I mean the barbershop."

"Oh, hello, Sheriff. This is Homer. Could I speak to Uncle Ulysses?"

"Well, he's playing pinochle right now," said the sheriff. "Anythin' I can tell 'im?"

"Yes," said Homer. "I pushed the button marked *Stop* on the doughnut machine, but the rings of batter keep right on dropping into the hot fat, and an automatic gadget keeps right on turning them over, and another automatic gadget keeps giving them a little push, and the doughnuts keep right on rolling down the little chute! It won't stop!"

"O.K. Wold the hire, I mean, hold the wire and I'll tell 'im." Then Homer looked over his shoulder and counted another twenty-one doughnuts roll down the little chute, all ready to eat. Then the sheriff said, "He'll be right over . . . Just gotta finish this hand."

"That's good," said Homer. "G'by, Sheriff."

The window was full of doughnuts by now, so Homer and Mr. Gabby had to hustle around and start stacking them on plates and trays and lining them up on the counter.

"Sure are a lot of doughnuts!" said Homer.

"You bet!" said Mr. Gabby. "I lost count at twelve hundred and two, and that was quite a while back."

People had begun to gather outside the lunchroom window, and someone was saying, "There are almost as many doughnuts as there are people in Centerburg, and I wonder how in tarnation Ulysses thinks he can sell all of 'em!"

Every once in a while somebody would come inside and buy some, but while somebody bought two to eat and a dozen to take home, the machine made three dozen more.

By the time Uncle Ulysses and the sheriff arrived and pushed through the crowd the lunchroom was a calamity of doughnuts! Doughnuts in the window, doughnuts piled high on the shelves, doughnuts stacked on plates, doughnuts lined up twelve deep all along the counter, and doughnuts still rolling down the little chute, just as regular as a clock can tick.

"Hello, Sheriff, hello, Uncle Ulysses, we're having a little trouble here," said Homer.

"Well, I'll be dunked! !" said Uncle Ulysses.

"Dernd ef you won't be when Aggy gits home," said the sheriff.

"Mighty fine doughnuts though. What'll you do with 'em all, Ulysses?"

Uncle Ulysses groaned and said, "What will Aggy say? We'll never sell 'em all."

Then Mr. Gabby, who hadn't said anything for a long time, stopped piling doughnuts and said, "What you need is an advertising man. Ya know what I mean? You got the doughnuts, ya gotta create a market . . . Understand? . . . It's balancing the demand with the supply . . . That sort of thing."

"Yep!" said Homer. "Mr. Gabby's right. We have to enlarge our market. He's an advertising sandwich man, so if we hire him, he can walk up and down in front of the theater and get the customers."

"You're hired, Mr. Gabby!" said Uncle Ulysses.

Then everybody pitched in to paint the signs and to get Mr. Gabby sandwiched between. They painted "SALE ON DOUGHNUTS" in big letters on the window too.

Meanwhile the rings of batter kept right on dropping into the hot fat, and an automatic gadget kept right on turning them over, and another automatic gadget kept right on giving them a little push, and the doughnuts kept right on rolling down the little chute, just as regular as a clock can tick.

"I certainly hope this advertising works," said Uncle Ulysses, wagging his head. "Aggy'll certainly throw a fit if it don't."

The sheriff went outside to keep order, because

there was quite a crowd by now — all looking at the doughnuts and guessing how many thousand there were, and watching new ones roll down the little chute, just as regular as a clock can tick. Homer and Uncle Ulysses kept stacking doughnuts. Once in a while somebody bought a few, but not very often.

Then Mr. Gabby came back and said, "Say, you know there's not much use o' me advertisin' at the theater. The show's all over, and besides almost everybody in town is out front watching that machine make doughnuts!"

"Zeus!" said Uncle Ulysses. "We must get rid of these doughnuts before Aggy gets here!"

"Looks like you will have ta hire a truck ta waul 'em ahay, I mean haul 'em away!!" said the sheriff, who had just come in. Just then there was a noise and a shoving out front, and the lady from the shiny black car and her chauffeur came pushing through the crowd and into the lunchroom.

"Oh, gracious!" she gasped, ignoring the doughnuts, "I've lost my diamond bracelet, and I know I left in here on the counter," she said, pointing to a place where the doughnuts were piled in stacks of two dozen.

"Yes, Ma'm, I guess you forgot it when you helped make the batter," said Homer.

Then they moved all the doughnuts around and

looked for the diamond bracelet, but they couldn't find it anywhere. Meanwhile the doughnuts kept rolling down the little chute, just as regular as a clock can tick.

After they had looked all around, the sheriff cast a suspicious eye on Mr. Gabby, but Homer said, "He's all right, Sheriff, he didn't take it. He's a friend of mine."

Then the lady said, "I'll offer a reward of one

hundred dollars for that bracelet! It really *must* be found! . . . it *really* must!"

"Now don't you worry, lady," said the sheriff. "I'll get your bracelet back!"

"Zeus! This is terrible!" said Uncle Ulysses. "First all of these doughnuts and then on top of all that, a lost diamond bracelet . . ."

Mr. Gabby tried to comfort him, and he said, "There's always a bright side. That machine'll probably run outta batter in an hour or two."

If Mr. Gabby hadn't been quick on his feet Uncle Ulysses would have knocked him down, sure as fate.

Then while the lady wrung her hands and said, "We must find it we *must!*" and Uncle Ulysses was moaning about what Aunt Agnes would say, and the sheriff was eyeing Mr. Gabby, Homer sat down and thought hard.

Before twenty more doughnuts could roll down the little chute he shouted, "SAY! I know where the bracelet is! It was lying here on the counter and got mixed up in the batter by mistake! The bracelet is cooked inside one of these doughnuts!"

"Why . . . I really believe you're right," said the lady through her tears. "Isn't that *amazing?* Simply *amazing!*"

"I'll be durn'd!" said the sheriff.

"OhH-h!" moaned Uncle Ulysses. "Now we have to break up all of these doughnuts to find it. Think of the *pieces!* Think of the *crumbs!* Think of what *Aggy* will say!"

"Nope," said Homer. "We won't have to break them up. I've got a plan."

So Homer and the advertising man took some cardboard and some paint and printed another sign. They put this sign in the window, and the sandwich man

FRESH DOUGHNUTS
2 FOR 5¢
WHILE THEY LAST
$ 100.⁰⁰ PRIZE
FOR FINDING
A BRACELET
INSIDE A DOUGHNUT
P.S. YOU HAVE TO GIVE THE
BRACELET BACK

wore two more signs that said the same thing and walked around in the crowd out front.

THEN . . . The doughnuts began to sell! *Everybody* wanted to buy doughnuts, *dozens* of doughnuts!

And that's not all. Everybody bought coffee to dunk the doughnuts in too. Those that didn't buy coffee bought milk or soda. It kept Homer and the lady and the chauffeur and Uncle Ulysses and the sheriff busy waiting on the people who wanted to buy doughnuts.

When all but the last couple of hundred doughnuts had been sold, Rupert Black shouted, "I GAWT IT! !" and sure enough . . . there was the diamond bracelet inside of his doughnut!

Then Rupert went home with a hundred dollars, the citizens of Centerburg went home full of doughnuts, the lady and her chauffeur drove off with the diamond bracelet, and Homer went home with his mother when she stopped by with Aunt Aggy.

As Homer went out of the door he heard Mr. Gabby say, "Neatest trick of merchandising I ever seen," and Aunt Aggy was looking sceptical while Uncle Ulysses was saying, "The rings of batter kept right on dropping into the hot fat, and the automatic gadget kept right on turning them over, and the other automatic gadget kept right on giving them a little push, and the doughnuts kept right on rolling down the little chute just as regular as a clock can tick — they just kept right on a-comin', an' a-comin', an' a-comin', an' a-comin'."

4

Mystery Yarn

Mystery Yarn

ONE fall afternoon Homer was whistling a little tune and raking up leaves from Uncle Ulysses' front lawn, and trying to decide whether to ask for his pay in cash or in doughnuts from Uncle Ulysses' lunchroom.

He'd just finished raking the leaves into a neat pile at the curb and was about to go find a match when the sheriff turned the corner in his car.

"Hi Sheriff! Do you have a match?" shouted Homer.

"Sure thing, Homer," said the sheriff as his car jerked to a stop. "That's a right smart pile o' leaves you got there. Lurning beaves, I mean burning leaves sure smell nice, don't they?" he said as he struck a match on his seat and lit the pile.

"Yep, Sheriff, and burning leaves always make me think of football and school," said Homer.

"And the county fair," added the sheriff. "That'll be along in a couple weeks. I'm gonna exhibit my chickens again this year. My white leghorns took a blue ribbon last fall. Well, I'll be seeing you, Homer," added the sheriff. Then he flicked a bit of ash off his sleeve, because he had his best Sunday suit on, climbed into his car, and drove to the end of the block. Homer watched while the sheriff got out of his car, straightened his tie, and started up Miss Terwilliger's front steps.

Miss Terwilliger, as anyone from Centerburg can tell you, is one of the town's best-known and best-loved citizens. She runs knitting classes and in years past has taught almost every woman in Centerburg how to knit. She is a familiar sight on Sundays, holidays, and at social functions, dressed in a robin's-egg-blue dress which she had knit years ago when she first started her knitting classes. In fact, Sundays and holidays did not seem complete without Miss Terwilliger in her robin's-egg-blue dress. You might think that a dress so old would look worn and out of style, but not Miss Terwilliger's. After church or after a party she changes to a housedress of simple cotton print and carefully hangs her favorite blue knit in a closet to save it for the next occasion. The matter of style doesn't bother Miss Terwilliger. If short skirts are the latest thing, she merely unravels a few inches from the bottom and the dress looks like the latest thing. Of course Miss Terwilliger saves the robin's-egg-blue yarn that she removes for, as she has so often remarked, "Longer skirts will be in style again in a year or two and then I'll have the right yarn to knit a few inches back onto the bottom of the skirt."

Miss Terwilliger is a *very* clever woman, and besides being an accomplished knitter she is a wonderful cook. Her fried chicken is famous for miles around Centerburg. It is only natural for such a woman to have many admirers, and two special ones, the sheriff and Homer's Uncle Telemachus. As long as Homer could remember, the sheriff had gone every Thursday, and Uncle Telemachus had gone every Sunday, to call on Miss Terwilliger and eat a chicken dinner. And it was no secret that both the sheriff and Uncle Telemachus wanted to marry Miss Terwilliger. She liked them both, but somehow she just couldn't seem to make up her mind.

Homer remembered that he had another job for this afternoon so he poked the fire some more to make it burn faster.

When the fire was out Homer put away the rake and hurried off to Uncle Telemachus' house.

Homer's Uncle Telly lived all by himself in a trim little house near the railroad. Homer's mother always said, "It's a shame that Uncle Telly had to live alone because he would make an ideal husband for some fine woman like Miss T." Aunt Aggy would always answer, "But I don't know how any fine woman could put up with his carryings on!"

By "carryings on" Aunt Aggy meant Uncle Telly's hobby of collecting string. Yes, Uncle Telly was a string saver, and he had saved string for years and years. He had quite a lot of it too. And every Thursday afternoon he would take all the pieces of string that he had collected during the week and wind them on his huge ball out in the garage. That was one of Homer's jobs on Thursdays, helping Uncle Telly wind string, because Uncle Telly had had a bit of rheumatism of late. You see, the ball of string was getting too large to wind without a lot of stooping and reaching.

Uncle Telly greeted Homer at the door, "Hello, Homer, we've got a lot to wind today!"

"That's good, Uncle Telly, I brought a few pieces from home too!"

They went out to the garage, and as Uncle Telly

looked at his ball of string he said with pride, "Another quarter inch and it'll be six feet across . . . biggest ball of string in the world."

"Well, I don't know, Uncle Telly," said Homer, "Freddy's been helping the sheriff wind his string down at the jail, and he says the sheriff's ball of string is just about six feet across too."

"Humph! I've heard tell that the sheriff winds his string loose, so's the ball looks bigger. Mine's wound *tight*," said Uncle Telly poking the ball, "and it's a lot longer than the sheriff's ball of string'll ever be."

"Yep! I guess you're right," said Homer, and he began winding the string while Uncle Telly tied the pieces together in double knots.

"Wind it tight," reminded Uncle Telly, "don't let anybody say that my string isn't wound right! I'll have none of this loose, sloppy, sheriff kind of winding on my ball o' string!"

Just as Homer and Uncle Telly were about finished there was a knock on the garage door, and when Uncle Telly opened the door there stood the sheriff and Judge Shank.

"Good day, Telemachus!" said the judge.

"Howdy, Telly," said the sheriff, trying to peer over Uncle Telly's shoulder and see the ball of string.

"Howdy, Judge," said Uncle Telly, and scowling

on the sheriff he said, "I didn't expect *you'd* be calling on *me* on a Thursday afternoon."

"Ahem, Telemachus," said the judge, "I just happened to stop in the knitting shop to drive my wife home when I met the sheriff. As you know Telly,— er, Telemachus — it is necessary to cut down expenses at the fair this year, and we cannot afford to have the trotting races that we have always had. The sheriff, who like myself is on the fair board, and who like yourself is a string saver, has suggested that he and you, Telemachus, enter into an event that could be held on the race track, and provide the diversion that the trotting races have . . ."

"Yep!" interrupted the sheriff, "I challenge you to unroll your string around the race track, just to prove once and for all that I've got more string than you have."

"Er, yes, to put it bluntly, that is the situation, Telemachus. I appeal to your sense of county pride. Do not spurn the offer. And then, of course, the winner will receive a prize . . ."

"I'll *do* it, by Zeus!" said Uncle Telly. "We'll see who's got the most string, Sheriff! Your ball might be just as big as mine, but it ain't wound tight." And to prove his point Uncle Telly gave his ball a kick and almost lost his balance.

"Very well, gentlemen," said the judge, "I shall..."

"Wait a minute, Judge," interrupted Uncle Telly, "I mean, I'll do it on one condition." (Uncle Telly was noted for driving a hard bargain and Homer wondered just what it would be.) "If I win this here contest, the sheriff has to promise to spend his Thursday afternoons out of town and give Miss Terwilliger a chance to make up her mind to marry me."

"Well," said the sheriff, "in that case, if *I* win you'll have to leave town on Sundays and give Miss Terwilliger a chance to make up her mind to marry *me!*"

"It's a deal," said Uncle Telly, and he and the sheriff shook hands for the first time in years (just to clinch the bargain of course).

"Very well, gentlemen," crooned the judge, "I shall judge this contest, and at our earliest convenience we will draw up a set of rules pertaining . . . Good day, Telemachus."

"G'by Telly," said the sheriff, "sorry I can't stay but I got an appointment"

Uncle Telly slammed the door on the sheriff and went back to tying knots.

"We'll see!" he said, and pulled the next knot so hard that he broke the string.

"Golly, Uncle Telly," said Homer. "That's going to be a swell contest. I hope you win the prize."

"Uhumpf! Prize or no prize we'll see who's got the most," said Uncle Telly, "and Miss Terwilliger will get a chance to make up her mind. That woman certainly can cook!" sighed Uncle Telly with a dreamy look. Then he busied himself with his knots and said, "Now mind you, Homer, wind it tight."

In the Friday night edition of the *Centerburg Bugle* Homer read a long article on the county fair, and a special anouncement about the contest to determine the world's champion string saver, and then the rules that Judge Shank had drawn up.

"Each contestant may appoint an assistant to help with the maneuvering of his ball of string."

"The balls of string shall be unwound, i.e., rolled around the county fair race track in a counterclockwise direction, starting from the judge's booth in front of the main grandstand."

"The ball of string reaching around the race track the greatest number of times shall be regarded as the winning string, and that string's owner shall be declared winner of the prize and of the title of World's Champion String Saver. The string shall be unwound for two hours every afternoon of the week of the fair, starting at two o'clock."

Homer read the rules and noticed that nothing was mentioned about the gentleman's agreement between the sheriff and Uncle Telly, but that sort of news travels fast in a town the size of Centerburg, and it wasn't long before practically everybody knew that the winner was *supposed* to have the hand of Miss Terwilliger in marriage.

Homer decided to go past Uncle Telly's house and see what he thought about the rules.

Homer couldn't help wondering what a woman who could cook fried chicken so well and who was as *clever* as Miss Terwilliger would do if *she* heard about the agreement.

Homer found Uncle Telly trying to figure out how many miles of string were wound on his ball. He was multiplying 3.1416 by the diameter, and after multiplying by several figures he asked Homer how many feet in a mile.

"Five thousand two hundred and eighty," said Homer.

Then Uncle Telly multiplied by four. Then he turned to Homer and said, "I figure there's enough string to go around that race track a hundred times. Yep! Twenty-five miles of string! Just let the sheriff beat that if he can!"

"Look, Uncle Telly, here comes the judge and the sheriff again, and look who's with them, *Miss Terwilliger!*"

Uncle Telly opened the door before the judge had a chance to knock, and the judge puffed in, followed by the sheriff and Miss Terwilliger.

"Ah, phuf! Ha, good day, Ha, Phuf! Telemachus, Haah! We have a new contestant for the title of World's Champion String Saver!" puffed the judge.

Miss Terwilliger blushed and giggled while Uncle Telly backed around to the other side of the room and raised his eyebrows at the sheriff in a way that asked, "Did *you* tell her about the agreement?" The sheriff shrugged his shoulders and wiggled his mustache that showed he was just as puzzled as Uncle Telly.

Miss Terwilliger (if she did know about the agreement) wasn't admitting it. "Isn't it *wonderful*," she said to Uncle Telemachus and the sheriff, "that we have *so* much in common?"

"Yes," she tittered, "I've been asavin' string for the past fifteen years! All of the colored yarn and odds and ends from knitting classes. I have a beautiful ball of yarn, all colors of the rainbow."

"Splendid!" said the judge, rubbing his hands together. "Simply splendid, Miss Terwilliger!"

"But Judge," interrupted Uncle Telly anxiously.

"Do you think," said the sheriff, nudging the judge, and winking frantically, "that a *woman* should enter into a sing of this thort, I mean thing of this sort?"

"Splendid!" continued the judge, ignoring these interruptions. "The American female is beginning to find her rightful place in the business and public life of this nation. The sheriff and Telemachus and I deeply appreciate your public spirit, Miss Terwilliger, and I'm sure that the county fair will be an unprecedented success."

"Come, Judge," said Miss Terwilliger with a smile, "I must get back to my knitting shop. Good-by Sheriff, good-by Telemachus, I'll see *you* on Sunday."

After the judge and Miss Terwilliger were gone the sheriff and Uncle Telly each accused the other of telling about the agreement. They finally calmed down and decided that the judge had double-crossed them with his fancy speech about "woman's rights."

"But Uncle Telly," said Homer, "there couldn't be *three* balls of string in the world as large as yours and the sheriff's."

"You're wrong, son!" said the sheriff with a sigh. "Her ball of string's *bigger* than mine! She's a clever woman, son, a *very* clever woman."

"If she wins," said Uncle Telly gloomily, "we'll be right back where we started from, waiting forever for her to make up her mind."

During the next week the whole county got excited about the contest to determine the world's champion string saver. Everybody started saving string for their favorite contestant. The ladies in Miss Terwilliger's knitting classes reported that Miss Terwilliger was knitting a brand-new dress for the occasion. When Homer's mother heard this, she called Aunt Aggy and said, "We should do something about Uncle Telly. You know how men are about clothes. They can hardly tell one dress or suit from another." The next day they dragged Uncle Telly downtown and picked out a nice new and very becoming plaid suit for him. The sheriff said, "If they're going to make a shashion fow, I mean fashion show, out of this thing I can dress up, too!" He sent away special delivery to Chicago and ordered an expertly fashioned double-breasted Hollywood model suit. On the day before the fair started, Homer went up to Miss Terwilliger's with the sheriff to see them take her ball of string out of the house. Mr. Olson, the carpenter, had to take out the side of the house because the ball just wouldn't go through the door. When the moving men rolled it out and on to the truck, the sheriff said, "That's as purty a ball a string as I've ever seen. It's got a toman's woutch! I mean a woman's touch!"

Just then Uncle Telly walked up and agreed, "It's

awful pretty, being all colors of the rainbow, but it ain't wound tight. It's so soft you can poke your fist right into it."

"Yes, but yarn stretches purty much," said the sheriff unhappily.

The day the fair opened, the grandstand was crowded and people stood halfway around the track when the contestants and their assistants started un-rolling their string. Miss Terwilliger's new pink dress and the sheriff's and Uncle Telly's new suits caused much favorable comment from the ladies present. The

men were more interested in the string, but as Homer's mother said, "They can hardly tell one dress or suit from another." Miss Terwilliger and the sheriff and Uncle Telly were hot and tired after the first two times around the track, and so were their assistants. So the judge had some of the regular county fair employees roll the balls while the contestants rode around the track alongside in the sheriff's car.

After the first afternoon's unrolling, Miss Terwilliger's ball measured 5'9"; the sheriff's measured

5′8¾″; Uncle Telly's 5′8″. Uncle Telly and the sheriff were very uneasy. At the end of the second day the sheriff's and Miss Terwilliger's 5′; Uncle Telly 4′11¹⁵⁄₁₆″. Uncle Telly felt a little better, and so did the sheriff.

The measurements at the end of the next to the last day of the fair were Uncle Telly and the sheriff running 16½″, and Miss Terwilliger only 12⅝″, and each contestant's ball of string had unrolled around the track ninety-nine times.

Uncle Telly and the sheriff were feeling pretty

confident now, and each one was sure of winning the title of world's champion string saver *and* the hand of the clever Miss Terwilliger.

On the last day of the contest everybody in Center County was on hand early. The contestants were going to roll their balls of string around the track themselves. The sheriff and Uncle Telly were all dressed up for the occasion, but Miss Terwilliger was not wearing her new knit dress. The ladies noticed right away that she was wearing the old robin's-egg-blue one that she had saved all these years. She started off carrying her ball in a gay little basket and a parasol to protect her from the autumn sun. She marched right off at two o'clock with her string trailing behind her.

Most everybody knew that Miss ·Terwilliger's ball was 3⅜" less across than the sheriff's or Uncle Telly's, and they admired her confidence and her spirit, but they all knew that she couldn't win.

Uncle T. and the sheriff, each feeling confident, were taking it slow. They watched each other like hawks, and they unwound their string right up against the fence and checked up on each other's knots. They hadn't even gotten a quarter of the way around when Miss Terwilliger was at the halfway mark.

Homer could see her walking right along wearing her robin's-egg-blue dress with the pink trim at the bottom, carrying her basket and the parasol to protect her from the autumn sun. The sheriff and Telly were halfway around still checking every knot and stretching their string as tight as they dared against the fence.

Now Miss Terwilliger was three quarters of the way around, still walking right along wearing her robin's-egg-blue blouse with the pink skirt, carrying her basket and the parasol to protect her from the autumn sun.

Uncle Telly shouted at the three-quarters mark, "I've won! The sheriff wound his string around a walnut! Mine's solid to the core!"

Everybody started shouting "Hurrah for Telly! Hurrah for Telly, the world's champion string saver!" And after the noise had died down people heard another shout, "I've won!" And then they noticed for the first time that Miss Terwilliger was standing right down in front of the grandstand wearing her dress with the robin's-egg-blue trim at the neck and sleeves, holding her basket and the parasol to protect her from the autumn sun.

The judge puffed down to where Miss Terwilliger was and held up the end of her string and shouted,

"I pronounce you the winner of the title of String Saving Champion of the World!"

Then everybody started cheering for Miss Terwilliger.

Uncle Ulysses and the sheriff trudged up and congratulated Miss Terwilliger, and told her how glad they were that she had won the championship. Everyone could see though that they were unhappy about having to wait forever for her to make up her mind — especially Uncle Telly.

Practically every woman who was there that day knew how the clever Miss Terwilliger had won the championship. They enjoyed it immensely and laughed among themselves, but they didn't give away the secret because they thought, "all's fair in love," and besides a woman ought to be allowed to make up her own mind.

There *might* have been a few *very* observing men, who like Homer, knew how she won. But they didn't say anything either, or maybe they just didn't get around to mentioning it before Miss Terwilliger finally decided to marry Uncle Telly the following week. It was a grand wedding, with the sheriff as best man.

Uncle Telemachus and his new wife left for Niagara Falls, while the guests at the reception were still drinking punch and eating wedding cake and doughnuts — not to mention fried chicken.

"That was a wandy dedding, I mean a dandy wedding!" said the sheriff to Homer while polishing off a chicken breast. He looked at the wishbone and sighed. Then after a minute he brightened and said, "But they've asked me to dinner every Thursday night!"

"You know, Homer," said the sheriff with a smile, "they'll be a very cappy houple, I mean happy couple, going through life savin' string together.

"Yep," said Homer, "I guess they're the undisputed champions now."

"Guess you're right, Homer, nobody'll *ever* get so much string saved on one ball as they have . . . Heck, I think I'll start savin' paper bags or bottle caps!"

5

Nothing New
Under the Sun
(Hardly)

Nothing New
Under the Sun
(Hardly)

AFTER the County Fair, life in Centerburg eases itself back to normal. Homer and the rest of the children concentrate on arithmetic and basketball, and the grown-ups 'tend to business and running the town in a peaceful, democratic way. Election time still being a month away, the Democrats and the Republicans are still speaking to each other. The Ladies' Aid hasn't anything to crusade about at the moment, and Uncle Ulysses hasn't bought any new-fangled equipment for his lunchroom recently. There is nothing for people to gossip about, or speculate on, or argue about.

There's always the weather, the latest books and movies, and ladies' hats. But, of course, that doesn't provide nearly enough to talk and think about for a whole month until election time. Uncle Ulysses, the sheriff, and the men around the barbershop usually run out of things to talk about toward the middle of the month. Sometimes during the mornings the conversation is lively. Like today, the sheriff came in beaming and said, "Well, I put on long ullen wonderwear, I mean woolen underwear, this morning."

"Soo?" said Uncle Ulysses. "Guess I'll have to ask Aggy to get mine out of mothballs this week."

"Humph," said the barber, "*I* wouldn't wear woolen underwear for anything on earth. It *itches!*"

Well, that was something to argue about for almost an hour. Then the subject changed to woolen socks, to shoes, to overshoes, to mud, to mud in roads, mud in barnyards and barns, chicken coops. Then there was a long pause. Only ten-thirty by the town hall clock, and conversation had already dwindled to nothing at all. Nothing to do but look out of the barbershop window.

"There goes Doc Pelly," said the barber, "I wonder who's sick?"

"Judge's wife having a fainting spell, maybe," suggested the sheriff.

"Colby's wife is expectin' a baby," said Uncle Ulysses. "I'll ask Aggy this noon, she'll know all about it."

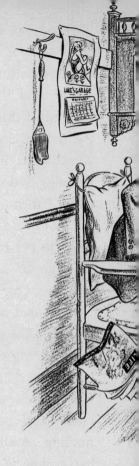

"There's Dulcey Dooner," said the sheriff. "He hasn't worked for three years," added the barber disapprovingly.

A few children came into view. "School's out for lunch," pronounced the sheriff.

The door opened and Homer came in saying, "Hello everybody. Uncle Ulysses, Aunt Aggy sent me over

to tell you to stir yourself over to the lunchroom and help serve blue-plate specials."

Uncle Ulysses sighed and prepared to leave. The sheriff cupped a hand behind his ear and said, "What's that?" Uncle Ulysses stopped sighing and everybody listened.

The noise (it was sort of a rattle) grew louder, and

then suddenly an old car swung into the town square. The sheriff, the barber, Uncle Ulysses, and Homer watched it with gaping mouths as it rattled around the town square once — twice — and on the third time slowed down and shivered to a stop right out front of Uncle Ulysses' lunchroom.

It wasn't because this car was old, old enough to be an *antique*; or because some strange business was built onto it; or that the strange business was covered with a large canvas. No, that wasn't what made Homer and the sheriff and Uncle Ulysses and the barber stare so long. It was the car's *driver*.

"Gosh what a beard!" said Homer.

"And what a head of hair!" said the barber. "That's a two-dollar cutting job if I ever saw one!"

"Could you see his face?" asked the sheriff.

"Nope," answered Uncle Ulysses, still staring across the square.

They watched the stranger untangle his beard from the steering wheel and go into the lunchroom.

Uncle Ulysses promptly dashed for the door, saying, "See you later."

"Wait for me!" the sheriff called, "I'm sort of hungry."

Homer followed and the barber shouted, "Don't forget to come back and tell me the news!"

"O.K., and if I bring you a new customer I get a commission."

The stranger was sitting at the far end of the lunch counter, looking very shy and embarrassed. Homer's Aunt Aggy had already served him a blue-plate special and was eyeing him with suspicion. To be polite, Homer and Uncle Ulysses pretended to be busy behind the counter, and the sheriff pretended to study the menu — though he knew every single word on it by heart. They just glanced in the stranger's direction once in a while.

Finally Uncle Ulysses' curiosity got the best of him and he sauntered down to the stranger and asked, "Are you enjoying your lunch? Is everything all right?"

The stranger appeared to be very embarrassed, and you could easily tell he was blushing underneath his beard and all his hair. "Yes, sir, it's a very good lunch," he replied with a nod. When he nodded a stray whisp of beard accidentally got into the gravy. This made him more embarrassed than ever.

Uncle Ulysses waited for the stranger to start a conversation, but he didn't.

So Uncle Ulysses said, "Nice day today."

The stranger said, "Yes, nice day," and dropped a fork. Now the stranger *really* was embarrassed. He

looked as though he would like to sink right through the floor.

Uncle Ulysses quickly handed the man another fork, and eased himself away, so as not to embarrass him into breaking a plate or falling off his stool.

After he finished lunch, the stranger reached into the pocket of his ragged, patched coat and drew out a leather moneybag. He paid for his lunch, nodded good-by, and crept out of the door and down the street with everyone staring after him.

Aunt Aggy broke the silence by bouncing on the marble counter the coin she had just received.

"It's good money," she pronounced, "but it looks as though it had been *buried* for *years!*"

"Shyest man I ever laid eyes on!" said Uncle Ulysses.

"Yes!" said the sheriff. "My as a shouse, I mean shy as a mouse!"

"Gosh what a beard!" said Homer.

"Humph!" said Aunt Aggy. "Homer, it's time you started back to school!"

By mid-afternoon every man, woman, and child in Centerburg had something to gossip about, speculate on, and argue about.

Who was this stranger? Where did he come from?

Where was he going? How long was his beard, and his hair? What was his name? Did he have a business? What could be on the back of his car that was so carefully covered with the large canvas?

Nobody knew. Nobody knew anything about the stranger except that he parked his car in the town parking space and was spending considerable time walking about town. People reported that he paused in his walking and whistled a few bars of some strange tune, a tune nobody had ever heard of. The stranger was shy when grown-ups were near, and he would cross the street or go around a block to avoid speaking to someone. However, he did not avoid children. He smiled at them and seemed delighted to have them follow him.

People from all over town telephoned the sheriff at the barbershop asking about the stranger and making reports as to what was going on.

The sheriff was becoming a bit uneasy about the whole thing. He couldn't get near enough to the stranger to ask him his intentions, and if he *did* ask the stranger would be too shy to give him an answer.

As Homer passed by the barbershop on his way home from school the sheriff called him in. "Homer," he said, "I'm gonna need your help. This stranger with the beard has got me worried. You see, Homer,

I can't find out who he is or what he is doing here in town. He's probably a nice enough fellow, just an individualist. But, then again, he might be a fugitive in disguise or something." Homer nodded. And the sheriff continued, "Now, what I want you to do is gain his confidence. He doesn't seem to be afraid of children, and you might be able to find out what this is all about. I'll treat you to a double raspberry sundae."

"It's a deal sheriff!" said Homer. "I'll start right now."

At six o'clock Homer reported to the sheriff. "The stranger seems like a nice person, Sheriff," Homer began. "I walked down Market Street with him. He wouldn't tell me who he is or what he's doing, but he did say he'd been away from people for a great many years. He asked me to recommend a place for him to stay, and I said the Strand Hotel, so that's where he went just now when I left him. I'll have to run home to dinner now, Sheriff, but I'll find out some more tomorrow. Don't forget about that raspberry sundae," said Homer.

"I won't," replied the sheriff, "and, Homer, don't forget to keep me posted on this fellow."

After Homer had gone, the sheriff turned to the barber and said, "Goll durnitt! We don't know one blessed thing about this fellow except that he's shy, and he's been away from people for quite a spell. For all we know he might be a fugitive, or a lunatic, or maybe one of these amnesia cases."

"If he didn't have so much hair I could tell in a second what kind of a fellow he is," complained the sheriff. "Yep! Just one look at a person's ears and *I* can *tell!*"

"Well," said the barber, "*I* judge people by their *hair*, and I've been thinking. This fellow looks like somebody I've heard about, or read about somewhere. Like somebody out of a book, you understand, Sheriff?"

"Well, yes, in a way, but I could tell you definite with a good look at his ears!" said the sheriff. "Here comes Ulysses, let's ask him what *he* thinks."

Uncle Ulysses considered a second and said, "Well, *I* judge a person by his *waistline* and his *appetite*. Now I'm not saying I'm right, Sheriff, because I couldn't tell about his waistline under that old coat, but judging from his appetite I'd say he's a sort of person that I've read about somewhere. I can't just put my finger on it. Seems as though it must have been in a book."

"U-m-m," said the sheriff.

Just then Tony the shoe repairman came in for a

haircut. After he was settled in the barber chair, the sheriff asked him what he thought about the mysterious stranger.

"Well, Sheriff, *I* judge everybody by their *feet* and their *shoes*. Nobody's worn a pair of gaiters like his for twenty-five years. It seems as though those shoes must have just up and walked right out of the pages of some old dusty book."

"There!" said the sheriff. "*Now* we're getting somewhere!"

He rushed to the phone and called Mr. Hirsh of the Hirsh Clothing Store, and asked, "Say, Sam, what do *you* think about this stranger? . . . Yes, the one bith the weard, I mean beard! . . . uh-huh . . . storybook clothes, eh? . . . Thanks a lot, Sam, good night."

Then he called the garage and said, "Hello, Luke, this is the sheriff talking. What do you make of this stranger in town . . . Yes? . . . literature, eh? Durn'd if I kin see how you can judge a man by the car he drives, but I'll take your word for it. Good night, Luke, and thanks a lot."

The sheriff looked very pleased with himself. He paced up and down and muttered, "Getting somewhere! Getting somewhere at last!" Then he surprised everyone by announcing that he was going over to the *library!*

In a few minutes he was back, his mustache twitching with excitement. "I've solved it!" he shouted. "The librarian knew right off just what book to look in! It's *Rip Van Winkle!* It's Rip Van Winkle this fellow's like. He must have driven up into the hills some thirty years ago and fell asleep, or got amnesia, or something!"

"Yeah! That's it!" agreed the barber along with Uncle Ulysses and the shoemaker.

Then Uncle Ulysses asked, "*But* how about that 'whatever-it-is' underneath the canvas on the back of his car?"

"Now look here, Ulysses," shouted the sheriff, "you're just trying to complicate my deduction! Come on, let's play checkers!"

Bright and early the next morning the Rip-Van-Winklish stranger was up and wandering around Centerburg.

By ten o'clock everyone was referring to him as "Old Rip," and remarking how clever the sheriff was at deducting things.

The sheriff tried to see what was under the canvas, but couldn't make head or tail of what it was. Uncle Ulysses peeked at it too and said, "Goodness only knows! But never mind, Sheriff. If anybody can find out what this thing is, Homer will do the finding!"

That same afternoon after school was dismissed Uncle Ulysses and the sheriff saw Homer strolling down the street with "Old Rip."

"Looks like he's explaining something to Homer," said the sheriff.

"Homer'll find out!" said Uncle Ulysses proudly. Then they watched through the barbershop window while the stranger took Homer across the square to the parking lot and showed him his car. He lifted one corner of the canvas and pointed underneath, while Homer looked and nodded his head. They shook hands and the stranger went to his hotel, and Homer headed for the barbershop.

"Did he talk?" asked the sheriff the minute Homer opened the door.

"What's his name?" asked Uncle Ulysses.

"What is he doing?" asked the barber.

"Yes, he told me everything!" said Homer. "It sounds just like a story out of a book!"

"Yes, son, did he get amnesia up in the hills?" asked the sheriff.

"Well no, not exactly, Sheriff, but he did *live* in the hills for the past thirty years."

"Well, what's he doing here now?" the barber demanded.

"I better start at the beginning," said Homer.

"That's a good idea, son," said the sheriff. "I'll take a few notes just for future reference."

"Well, to begin with," Homer started, "his name is Michael Murphy — just plain Michael Murphy. About thirty years ago he built himself a small vacation cabin out in the hills, some place on the far side of the state forest reserve. Then, he liked living in the cabin so much he decided to live there all of the time. He packed his belongings on his car and moved out to the hills."

"He cided ta be a dermit?" asked the sheriff.

"Not exactly a *hermit*," Homer continued. "But yesterday was the first time that he came out of the hills and saw people for thirty years. That's why he's so shy."

"Then he's moving back to civilization," suggested Uncle Ulysses.

"That comes later," said Homer, "I've only told as far as twenty-nine years ago."

"Can't you skip a few years, son, and get to the point?" demanded the sheriff.

"Nope! Twenty-nine years ago," Homer repeated firmly, "Mr. Murphy read in an almanac that if a man can make a better mousetrap than anybody else, the world will beat a path to his house — even if it is way out in the hills.

"So-o-o he started making *mousetraps*."

There was a pause, and then the sheriff said, "Will you repeat that again, son?"

"I said, Mr. Murphy started making *mousetraps*. He made good ones too — the very best — and when one of Mr. Murphy's traps caught a mouse, that was the end of that mouse for all time."

The sheriff forgot all about taking notes as Homer continued, "But nobody came to buy the traps. But that was just as well, you see, because twenty-eight years ago Mr. Murphy began to feel *sorry* for the mice. He came to realize that he would have to change his whole approach. He thought and thought, and finally he decided to build mousetraps that wouldn't hurt the mice.

"He spent the next fifteen years doing research on what was the pleasantest possible way for a mouse to be caught. He discovered that being caught to music pleased mice the most, even more than cheese. Then," said Homer, "Mr. Murphy set to work to make a *musical* mousetrap."

"That wouldn't hurt the mice?" inquired Uncle Ulysses.

"That wouldn't hurt the mice," Homer started. "It was a long, hard job too, because first he had to build an organ out of reeds that the mice liked the sound of, and then he had to compose a tune that the mice couldn't possibly resist. Then he incorporated it all into a mousetrap . . ."

"That wouldn't hurt the mice?" interrupted the barber.

"That wouldn't hurt the mice," Homer went on. "The mousetrap caught mice, all right. The only trouble was, it was too big. What with the organ and all, and sort of impractical for general use because somebody had to stay around and pump the organ."

"Yes, I can see that wouldn't be practical," said Uncle Ulysses, stroking his chin —"But with a small electric motor . . ."

"But he solved it, Uncle Ulysses! The whole idea seems very practical after you get used to it. He decided since the trap was too large to use in a house, he would fasten it onto his car, which he hadn't used for so long anyway. Then he could drive it to a town and make a bargain with the mayor to remove all the mice. You see he would start the musical mousetrap to working, and drive up and down the streets and alleys. Then all of the mice would run out of the houses to get themselves caught in this trap that plays music that no mouse ever born can possibly resist. After the trap is full of mice, Mr. Murphy drives them out past the city limits, somewhere where they can't find their way home, and lets them go."

"Still without hurting them?" suggested the barber.

"Of course," said Homer.

The sheriff chewed on his pencil, Uncle Ulysses stroked on his chin, and the barber ran his fingers through his hair.

Homer noticed the silence and said, "I guess the idea *is* sort of startling when you first hear about it. But if a town has a water truck to sprinkle streets, and a street-sweeping truck to remove dirt, why shouldn't they, maybe, just hire Mr. Murphy's musical mousetrap once in a while to remove mice?"

Uncle Ulysses stroked his chin again and then said, "By gum! This man Murphy is a genius!"

"I told Mr. Murphy that *you* would understand, Uncle Ulysses!" said Homer with a grin. "I told him the mayor was a friend of yours, and you could talk him into anything, even hiring a musical mousetrap."

"Whoever heard of a micical moostrap!" said the sheriff.

"That doesn't hurt the *mice!*" added the barber as Homer and Uncle Ulysses went off arm in arm to see the mayor.

It scarcely took Uncle Ulysses and Homer half an hour to convince the mayor that Mr. Murphy's musical mousetrap should be hired to rid Centerburg of mice. While Uncle Ulysses chatted on with the mayor, Homer dashed over to the hotel to fetch Mr. Murphy.

Homer came back with the bearded inventor and introduced him to the mayor and to Uncle Ulysses. The mayor opened a drawer of his desk and brought out a bag of jelly beans. "Have one," he said to Mr. Murphy, to sort of break the ice and make his shy visitor feel at home. Mr. Murphy relaxed and answered the mayor's questions without blushing too much.

"How do we know this *thing of a jig* of yours will do what you say it will?" asked the mayor.

Mr. Murphy just whistled a few bars *"Tum tidy ay dee"* and a couple of mice jumped right out of the mayor's desk!

"Of course," Homer explained, "the mice come *quicker* and get *removed* when the mousetrap plays that tune through the streets. Mr. Murphy guarantees to remove every single mouse from Centerburg for only thirty dollars."

"It's a bargain!" said the mayor, "I wondered where my jelly beans were disappearing to!" and he shook hands with Mr. Murphy. Then he proclaimed Saturday as the day for demousing Centerburg. By this time everyone knew that the shy stranger's name was Michael Murphy, but people still spoke of him as Rip

Van Winkle (Rip for short), because of the sheriff's deduction. Everybody talked about the musical mousetrap (that didn't hurt the mice) and the mayor's demousing proclamation.

The children, especially, were looking forward to the great event. They watched with interest while Mr. Murphy went over his car and his musical trap to be sure everything was in perfect working order. Homer and Freddy and most of the other children were planning to follow the trap all around town Saturday, and see the mice come out and get caught in Michael Murphy's musical trap.

"Gosh, Homer, said Freddy, "let's follow him until he lets them loose out in the country! That *will* be a sight, seeing all those mice let loose at once!"

"Well, Freddy, I've been thinking it might not be a good idea to follow the mousetrap past the city limits," said Homer to Freddy's surprise.

"You know, Freddy, I've been over at the library reading up on mice and music — music can do funny things sometimes. It can soothe savage beasts and charm snakes and *lots* of things. If we're going to follow this musical trap till the mice are let loose, we better make some plans."

Homer and Freddy spent all Friday recess period making plans. They decided that all the children should meet in the school yard before the demousing started on Saturday. They arranged a signal, thumbs up, if everything was going along all right, and thumbs down if anyone was in trouble.

"It's just to be on the safe side," Homer explained.

Saturday dawned a beautiful crisp fall day, fine weather for the grand demousing of Centerburg. Mr. Michael Murphy came forth from the Strand Hotel, and after carefully slinging his long gray beard over his shoulder he cranked his car and warmed up the engine. He carefully removed the canvas covering from the musical mousetrap and ever so painstakingly arranged the spiral ramps and runways so that no mouse, no matter how careless, could stub a toe or bump a nose. He then climbed behind the steering wheel and the musical mousetrap was underway!

A loud cheer arose from the crowd of children as Mr. Murphy yanked a lever and the reed organ started to play. Even before the cheering stopped the mice began to appear!

Through the streets of Centerburg rolled Mr. Michael Murphy and his musical mousetrap. The mice came running from every direction! Fat, dough-nut-fed mice from Uncle Ulysses lunchroom, thin mice from the churches, ordinary mice from houses

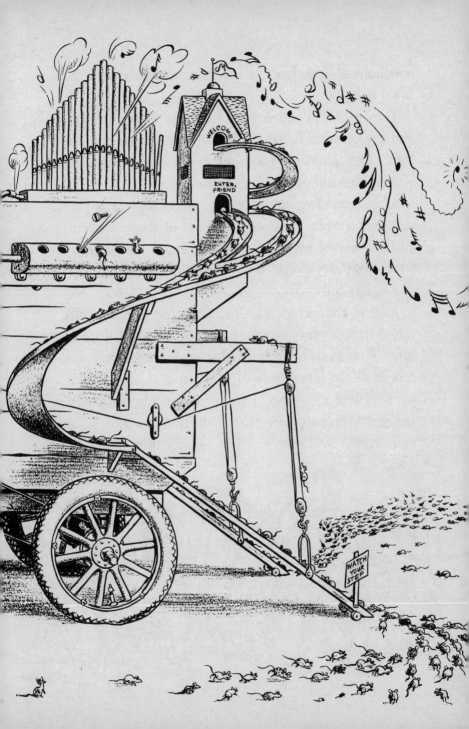

and homes, mice from the stores, and mice from the town hall.

They all went running up the ramps and runways, and disappeared in Michael Murphy's musical mousetrap. The children followed behind, enjoying the whole thing almost as much as the mice.

After traveling down every street in town, the procession came to a stop in front of the town hall, and the mayor came out and presented Mr. Murphy with his thirty-dollar fee — thirty bright, crisp new one-dollar bills.

Just as the mayor finished counting out the bills into Mr. Murphy's hand, the sheriff stepped up and said, "Mr. Murphy, I hope this won't embarrass you too much, in fact I hate to mention it at all, but this here misical moostrap, I mean mouse trap of yours, has got a license plate that is thirty years old . . . A *new* license will cost you just exactly thirty dollars."

Mr. Murphy blushed crimson under his beard. "It's the law, you know, and *I* can't help it!" apologized the sheriff.

Poor Mr. Murphy, poor *shy* Mr. Murphy! He handed his thirty dollars to the sheriff, took his new license plates and crept down the city hall steps. He climbed into his car and drove slowly away toward the edge of town, with the musical mousetrap playing its reedy music. The children followed along to see Mr. Murphy release all of the mice.

"I really hated to do that, Mayor," said the sheriff as the procession turned out of sight on route 56A. "It's the law you know, and if I hadn't reminded him he might have been arrested in the next town he visits." There's no telling how this demousing would have ended if the children's librarian hadn't come shouting "Sheriff! Sheriff! Quick! *We guessed the wrong book!*"

"What?" shouted the sheriff and the mayor and Uncle Ulysses.

"Yes!" gasped the children's librarian, "not *Rip Van Winkle*, but *another* book, *The Pied Piper of Hamelin!*"

"Geeminy Christmas!" yelled the sheriff, "and almost every child in town is followin' him this very minute!"

The sheriff and the librarian and the mayor and Uncle Ulysses all jumped into the sheriff's car and roared away after the procession. They met up with the children just outside the city limits. "Come back! Turn around, children!" they shouted.

"I'll treat everybody to a doughnut!" yelled Uncle Ulysses.

The children didn't seem to hear, and they kept right on following the musical mousetrap.

"The music must have affected their minds," cried the librarian.

"Sheriff, we can't lose all these children with election time coming up next month!" mourned the mayor. "Let's give Murphy another thirty dollars!"

"That's the idea," said Uncle Ulysses. "Drive up next to him, Sheriff, and I'll hand him the money."

The sheriff's car drew alongside the musical mousetrap, and Uncle Ulysses tossed a wad of thirty dollar bills onto the seat next to the shy Mr. Murphy.

"Please don't take them away!" pleaded the librarian.

"Come, Murphy, let's be reasonable," shouted the mayor.

Mr. Murphy was very flustered, and his steering was distinctly wobbly.

Then the sheriff got riled and yelled at the top of his lungs, *"Get 'em low! Get 'em go! Durnit, Let 'em go!"*

And that's exactly what Mr. Murphy did. He let them go. He pulled a lever and every last mouse came tumbling out of the bottom of the musical mousetrap. And *such* a *sight* it was, well worth walking to the city limits to see. The mice came out in a torrent. The reedy organ on the musical mousetrap stopped playing, and the squeaking of mice and the cheering of children filled the air.

The torrent of mice paused, as if sensing direction, and then each Centerburg mouse started off in a straight, straight line to his own Centerburg mouse-hole. Mr. Murphy didn't pause. He stepped on the gas, and the musical mousetrap swayed down the road. The mayor, the children's librarian, the sheriff, Uncle Ulysses, and the children watched as it grew smaller and smaller and finally disappeared.

Then Uncle Ulysses remembered the children. He turned around and noticed them grinning at each other and holding their thumbs in the air. They paid no attention whatever when they were called!

"That music has pixied these children!" he moaned.

"No, it hasn't, Uncle Ulysses," said Homer who had just come up. "There's not a thing the matter with them that Doc Pelly can't cure in two shakes! Just to be on the safe side, Freddy and I asked Doc Pelly to come down to the school yard this morning and put cotton in all the children's ears. You know, just like Ulysses — not you, Uncle Ulysses, but the ancient one, the one that Homer wrote about. Not me, but the ancient one."

"You mean to say Doc Pelly is mixed up in this?"

asked the mayor.

"Yes, he thought it was awfully funny, our being so cautious."

Uncle Ulysses laughed and said, "Round 'em up and we'll all go down to the lunchroom for doughnuts and milk."

"Sheriff," said the mayor, "with election time coming next month *we* gotta put our heads together and cook up a good excuse for spending sixty dollars of the taxpayers' money."

6

Wheels of Progress

Wheels of Progress

"I CAN'T go fishing today, Freddy," said Homer, "because I'm helping Uncle Ulysses down at the lunchroom. Seems as though the fish ought to be biting on a day like this."

"Do you think your Uncle Ulysses could use an extra helper today, Homer? Because it isn't imperative that I hafta go fishing. I just thought, if you weren't busy—"

"Gosh, Freddy! Uncle Ulysses would like it. He always says the more help the merrier, but Aunt Aggie is a 'too many cooks spoil the soup' sort of person and she says she's sick and tired of seeing more people behind the counter than in front of it."

"O.K., Homer," said Freddy with a sigh. "I'll see you tomorrow. Bring me a couple of doughnuts if you can."

When Homer entered the lunchroom, there was Uncle Ulysses puttering with one of his labor-saving devices.

"Hello, Homer!" he said, "you're just in time to help me adjust the timing mechanism in this electric toaster. When you want the toast to come out *light* brown it comes out *nut* brown, and vicey versey."

Homer and Uncle Ulysses tinkered with the toaster and then tried several pieces of toast. Then they tinkered with the mechanism some more.

"How is the doughnut machine working these days, Uncle Ulysses?" asked Homer.

"Just fine," said Uncle Ulysses. "We're selling more doughnuts than ever, with that new recipe. I suppose you've heard about the lady who gave us the old family recipe — the lady who lost her bracelet in the batter? She lives in Centerburg now. She's Naomi Enders, a great-great-great-granddaughter of Ezekiel Enders, the first settler of Centerburg. She inherited all of the Enders property when old Luke Enders died. She owns the Mill and the Patent Medicine Company now, and is living in the big Enders Homestead at the edge of town. She stops by for doughnuts almost every day; one of my best customers, she is."

"Yep," said Homer, "the judge mentioned that she had come to live in Centerburg. He said that she was a 'Public-Spirited Person' and would be 'An Addition to the Town.'"

"She appreciates good food," said Uncle Ulysses, tasting a piece of nut-brown toast, "and what's more she has a receptive mind — receptive to the new devices, and up-and-coming ideas."

A car stopped out front and Uncle Ulysses peered out and said, "Here she comes now, Homer, better start packing two dozen doughnuts to take out."

"Good afternoon," said Miss Enders. "Hello, Homer. I haven't seen you since the night my bracelet disappeared!"

"Hello, Miss Enders," said Homer. "How do you like living in Centerburg?"

"I think it's a marvelous town, simply marvelous!" replied Miss Enders. "I've been thinking of what I could do to show my appreciation for the way the people of Centerburg have received me. Everyone has been so kind, simply marvelous! I've just been talking to the judge, and he has informed me that there is a growing housing shortage and that people are having difficulty finding places to live. I've decided that a nice way of showing my appreciation would be to build a few homes on the family property. They could be replicas of the Enders Homestead — a sort of monument — and I could rent them reasonably to deserving families."

"Uhm-m-m!" said Uncle Ulysses, stroking his chin. "Good idea, Miss Enders, good idea."

Homer agreed, and while he counted out two dozen doughnuts he thought of the fun there would be, walking rafters and joists in the new houses.

Uncle Ulysses stopped stroking his chin and said, "I'll tell you, Miss Enders, it wouldn't do any harm to have more *modern* houses than the Homestead."

"Of course," said Miss Enders, "modern plumbing."

Uncle Ulysses went back to stroking his chin and saying, "Uhm-m-m."

"And modern kitchen equipment," said Miss Enders, as though she knew *that* would bring instant approval from Uncle Ulysses.

"Uhm-m-m," said Uncle Ulysses, and stroked his chin from left to right.

Finally he cleared his throat and said, "These are changing times, Miss Enders, and we're living in an age of ideas and production genius. Now take the way they *used* to make doughnuts for instance—each one cooked by hand, and all that time and bother.

Now we have this wonderful machine – makes dough-nuts just like that!" said Uncle Ulysses, snapping his fingers. Snap! Snap! Snap!

"It's marvelous," said Miss Enders, "simply mar-velous!"

"Uhm-m-m," continued Uncle Ulysses. "Now take the matter of houses. The way they *used* to build houses — saw up each board, hammer in nails one at a time, every little shingle and door knob fastened on by hand. But *now*," said Uncle Ulysses, "with up-and-coming ideas and modern production genius houses can be built just like this here machine makes doughnuts —" and he made a broad sweep with his right arm. "That's the principle!" pronounced Uncle Ulysses, while Miss Enders and Homer gazed in wide-eyed wonder.

"That's the principle that Henry Ford applied to making autos. Yep! Autos are mass-produced like doughnuts; ships are built like doughnuts; airplanes and refrigerators, and now *houses*. Yessiree, the *modern* houses ought to be mass-produced — just like cars or ships or planes. Yessiree! Mass-produced, just like that there machine makes doughnuts!" and here Uncle Ulysses snapped his fingers, snap, snap, snap, snap, and said, "Houses, just like that! . . ." Snap!

He then stopped waving his arms and talking, and

appeared startled that he had talked so much and with such wisdom. He started stroking his chin again, while Miss Enders, quite visibly impressed was murmuring "Marvelous! Simply marvelous!"

Homer counted the two dozen doughnuts again.

"Of course," said Uncle Ulysses, "it wouldn't be *quite* as fast or as easy as making doughnuts, but with assembly lines and sub-assembly lines, and power presses and a touch of ingenuity — that's your recipe. You can bake a house in twenty-four hours flat! . . ." Snap!

"Build," corrected Homer.

"Simply marvelous!" said the receptive Miss Enders. "*Simply marvelous!*"

Homer had heard Uncle Ulysses' pet theories before, and the sheriff and the boys over at the barbershop all had heard Uncle Ulysses carry on about the up-and-coming ideas. In fact, arguing about Uncle Ulysses' pet theories had broken up as many pinochle and checker games as arguing about the World Series and Woman Suffrage put together. That was all that ever happened, though, *arguing*. But that afternoon in the lunchroom was different.

Miss Enders was *receptive* to Uncle Ulysses up-and-comingness, and, what's more, she had the money

to be receptive and up and coming *with*. Almost before the week was up Miss Enders and the judge (who was her lawyer) and Uncle Ulysses were having conferences. They wrote letters to Detroit, where they have assembly lines and subassembly lines and huge presses that can stamp out the whole side of a house just as easily as stamping out the body of a car or a section of a ship. They hired up-and-coming designers and landscape architects, too. Almost before she knew it, Miss Enders had made arrangements for *one hundred houses* — a whole *suburb!* — to be built on the estate around the Enders Homestead. As Uncle Ulysses so wisely put it, "It don't pay to go to all the trouble of mixing batter and getting the machine hot for two or three doughnuts. Might just as well make a *hundred* while you're at it!"

The plans were finally finished and the arrangements all made. The workmen arrived at the Enders estate, and then things really began to happen. The trees were chopped down and hauled away, the land was leveled by huge tractors, and streets were laid out around the old Homestead in a day or two. Then power diggers arrived right on schedule and dug one foundation right after another.

Homer drove over to the suburb with Uncle Ulysses and Miss Enders to see how things were going. Uncle

Ulysses watched the dirt fly and counted as the machines dug foundations. "Seventy-two, seventy-three, seventy-four. I tell you, my boy," he said to Homer, "you are witnessing the beginning of a new era in city planning and housing! Eighty, eighty-one . . . Why, tomorrow they will start to build; by the end of the week people will *live* here."

"Simply marvelous," exclaimed Miss Enders. "Just think. Last week there were only grass and trees and squirrels on this spot!"

Everything happened right on schedule, just as Uncle Ulysses had predicted.

Huge trucks and trailers drove along the streets, unloaded subassembled sides and floors and roofs of houses, all complete to the last window, doorknob, light bulb, and hot and cold water. It was just a matter of an hour or so for the workmen to fasten the sides and floors together and put on the roof.

As the Centerburg newspaper said in an editorial, "Truly we are witnessing a modern miracle. Little did Ezekiel Enders know when he founded this town one hundred and fifty years ago that such things as this would come to pass. The *Centerburg Bugle* is sponsoring a 'One Hundred and Fifty Years of Centerburg Progress Week' to be celebrated when this new part of town is finished. Judge Shank and Miss Enders are heading the Committee and handling the celebration. Anyone wishing to take part in the Pageant, please get in touch with the Committee or call at the *Bugle* Office."

Toward the end of the week a truckload of mass-produced furniture was moved into every house. Each front yard had its own climbing rose bush, two dwarf cedars, and maple trees, all planted and sodded round about. Each back yard had its mass-produced ash can, birdhouse complete with weather vane, and revolving clothesline. In fact modern production genius had thought of everything: sheets, towels, pillowcases, and a print of *Whistler's Mother* for over every fireplace. The houses were *complete* and ready to be moved into. They *were* moved into too! As you can see, moving in was little more than signing a paper and hanging your hat on the mass-produced hanger in the hall.

Uncle Ulysses was very busy these days attending to last minute details. The judge and Miss Enders were working frantically on the pageant for "One Hundred and Fifty Years of Centerburg Progress Week."

Uncle Ulysses attended to street lights and fire plugs, and one afternoon he met Homer on the street and asked, "Have you seen Dulcey Dooner around lately? I have to make arrangements to have street signs put up in the new suburb. Have you heard, Homer," he added proudly, "they're going to name one of the streets *Ulysses Terrace* in honor of me!"

"Why yes, Uncle Ulysses, I just saw Dulcey coming out of the cigar store across the square."

Uncle Ulysses and Homer hurried back to catch Dulcey Dooner, the town's street sign putter-upper.

"Hi there, Dulcey," shouted Uncle Ulysses. "I'd like to discuss a matter of business with you . . . Street signs, street signs for our new suburb!"

Dulcey turned around and said, "Hi Ulysses. Hi Homer. I've been hearing about this new part of town."

"It's a great thing for Centerburg." said Uncle Ulysses. "We'll need about seventy street signs,

Dulcey. The signs are all made, and they can be fastened to the corner lampposts. We'll pay a dollar a sign to have them put up."

"Well," said Dulcey, "that's only seventy dollars, and I'm not so sure that the Street Sign Putter-Uppers Union would agree to that."

"But Dulcey, there are almost thirty other signs to put up. That makes *one hundred dollars*. The union surely wouldn't object to that!"

"Yes," said Dulcey, "I know, but I can't fasten the signs onto the corner street lamps, because the Street Sign Putter-Uppers Union rules say that any 'street sign put up by a brother of this here Union must be fastened to a post erected by a brother of this here Union, set in a post hole dug by a brother of this here Union.' The complete union rate is ten dollars a street sign for the hole, post and sign."

"But we don't need *another* post on each corner. The lampposts will do very well," said Uncle Ulysses, growing frantic.

"Couldn't you arbitrate or something?" suggested Homer.

"Yes," agreed Uncle Ulysses, "I'll write to the president of your union and ask him . . ."

"Well, Ulysses," said Dulcey proudly, "*I'm* the president of the Street Sign Putter-Uppers Union. I'm the secretary-treasurer too. Ya see, Ulysses, I make all the union rules, pay all the dues (and collect them too), so what I say goes."

"But certainly you must have up-and-coming ideas like the rest of the citizens of Centerburg. There must be some compromise. Say five dollars a sign!"

"Nope," said Dulcey firmly, "it's ten dollars or nothing. Street sign putter-upping is a seasonal occupation, and I can't run the union on five bucks a sign!"

"Well," sighed Uncle Ulysses, "I guess we'll have to make other arrangements."

"If you make other arrangements, the union will have to picket your new part of town," said Dulcey.

Uncle Ulysses began to get mad. Homer hadn't seen him so upset since the night the doughnut machine wouldn't stop making doughnuts. He shouted something about Dulcey being a wrench in the wheels of progress, but Dulcey just repeated, "Ten dollars apiece, or strike."

Homer had to rush off before the argument was finished, because tonight (Friday) was the dress rehearsal of the pageant. Homer and Freddy and a couple of their friends were taking the part of Indians. They were going to be powdered all over with cocoa, striped with mercurochrome, and draped with towels around their middles.

Homer had to get to rehearsal right on the dot because he started the pageant by rubbing two sticks together to make a fire. Most of the pageant was historical, all about Ezekiel Enders and the founding of Centerburg. The organist of the African Baptist Church wrote the words and music for a long choral work, which the choir was going to sing all the while the pageant was being acted.

The rehearsal went very well. The choir was in good voice, and the citizens taking the parts of Ezekiel Enders and the early settlers performed just right. So did Homer and Freddy and the boys, except for their scalping scene, which had to be modified somewhat. The grand One Hundred and Fifty Years of Centerburg Progress Week was drawing near!

Meanwhile every one of the hundred houses had been rented to a deserving family.

Homer hadn't seen Uncle Ulysses in the past two days, but he knew he must be having his troubles. For one thing, the street signs still hadn't been put up.

As all of the streets looked alike, this caused some slight confusion to the deserving tenants. The fact that all of the hundred houses looked as alike as a hundred doughnuts added to this slight confusion. However the deserving tenants soon found that by counting houses from the Enders Homestead, they

could find their way home without much trouble. Freddy's aunt was one of the deserving tenants, and when Freddy and Homer called on her they had to count three houses down from the Enders' Homestead, six houses to the left, and the next house to the right was Freddy's aunt's. "It's a sort of a game," Freddy said to Homer.

Miss Enders was proud as Punch of her suburb. She decided to call it *Enders' Heights*, even though it was flat as a board. "It's marvelous," she said. "Simply marvelous!"

The only thing she wasn't happy about was that her house (The Homestead) seemed out of place,

sitting as it did in the middle of Enders' Heights.
Uncle Ulysses and the judge agreed that The Homestead did stand out like a sore thumb. They decided
that the best thing to do was move it away and build
another house there. It would have to be done quickly
so as to be complete by the time the pageant started,
that night. Uncle Ulysses late that day ironed out his
difficulty with Dulcey Dooner. Dulcey, for ten dollars
a sign, and a slight increase for overtime and having
to miss the pageant, agreed to have all the street signs
up by the time the pageant ended that night.

By eight o'clock the town square was crowded.
Everyone was there to celebrate the One Hundred

and Fifty Years of Centerburg Progress Week. Promptly at eight-fifteen Homer, as an Indian, started rubbing his sticks together to make a fire. After the fire was lighted, Homer, Freddy, and the other Indians left the stage.

The judge was commentator, and while the pageant was being acted in pantomime he read from the *History of Enders County*. The African Baptist Choir chanted in the background.

"Ezekiel Enders," boomed the judge, "set foot on American soil owning but two shillings, an extra shirt, and a formula for making a Cough Syrup and Elixir of Life Compound that had been handed down in the Enders family for years. Soon after arriving he took himself a wife, and was soon the father of a child." The judge looked up from the text and said, "This child was destined to be the grandfather of our own dear public-spirited citizen, Miss Naomi Enders." (Loud applause.) The judge continued: "Hearing of the fertile lands to the West, Ezekiel Enders packed his beloved wife and son and his formula into a covered wagon, and with a few brave followers started toward the West . . . The Land of Plenty. Trouble seemed to follow Ezekiel and his brave little band. Their food ran out, game was scarce, and one day they found themselves in the wilderness with no food to sustain life. It was on that day, one hundred and fifty years ago, on this very spot, that Ezekiel found forty-two pounds of edible fungus growing in the forest." (Here the African Baptist Choir sang out in full rich harmony)

> "Forty-two pounds of edible fungus
> In the wilderness a-growin'
> Saved the settlers from starvation,
> Helped the founding of this nation.
> Forty-two pounds of edible fungus
> In the wilderness a-growin'."

"Ezekiel took it to be a sign, so he and his followers founded a town on this spot. Ezekiel purchased two thousand acres of land from the Indians with a jug of Cough Syrup. They named the town *Edible Fungus*, and they tilled the land and prospered.

"Peace and prosperity rested like a benediction on the brave company until the Indians, having become addicted to Ezekiel's Cough Syrup and Elixir of Life Compound, rose in arms against them. Ezekiel buried his supply of the Compound in his cabin floor and guarded his Formula and his loved ones. In time the Indian uprising was quelled, and once more peace and prosperity came to Edible Fungus."

The choir sang:

> "Peace again in Edible Fungus
> Prosperity now rests among us."

"We now skip seventy-five years, to the time Ezekiel's son founded the Enders Patent Medicine Company and the Mill. The town had grown and prospered, and its name was changed from Edible Fungus to *Centerburg*."

(Loud cheering)

The rest of the pageant was very symbolic. Uncle Telly's wife, the former Miss Terwilliger, was dressed as The Spirit of Water Power. Miss Enders was The Spirit of Cough Syrup and Vitamin B Compound. The Ladies of the Grange were the Spirits of Agriculture.

The judge then told the story of the building of Enders Heights, while Aunt Aggy (Uncle Ulysses' wife), dressed as The Spirit of Progress and Up-and-comingness, hovered on the platform.

The celebration ended with a torchlight procession to Enders Heights.

But lo! Once again the peace and comfort of Edible Fungus, alias Centerburg, i.e. Enders Heights, was threatened!

The street signs were not up! The Enders Homestead had been moved!

Another house, like all the others, stood in its place. One hundred and one houses, all alike, down to the last doorknob! Each with its climbing rose bush, two dwarf cedars, and maple tree sodded round about. Just as alike as one hundred and one doughnuts, and *nothing*, no *nothing* to count from to find out which was which and whose was whose. There was a mad scramble, with much shouting, with the deserving tenants trying frantically to find out which house was which.

The shouting broke into a chant of "We want Dulcey. We want Dulcey. We want Dulcey Doooooooooner."

Uncle Ulysses could do nothing. He had given his plans and diagrams to Dulcey — so the signs could be put up correctly. Miss Enders had another set of plans and diagrams in one of her handbags or somewhere, but it couldn't be located at the moment.

"We want Dulcey Dooner!" the crowd roared.

The judge began to worry about the reputation of the town. "There has never been a lynching in Enders County," he said.

It was Homer and Freddy who finally found Dulcey, quietly sleeping on a street corner that was just

like all the other street corners, except for the post hole Dulcey'd started to dig.

The crowd gathered around. They shook and prodded Dulcey, shouting "Where are the plans?"

"Where are the diagrams?"

"Where is Ulysses Terrace?"

"Where is Ezekiel Road?"

It was soon apparent that Dulcey was more than just *asleep*. He finally opened one eye and answered all questions the same: a shrug of the shoulders, "I dunno," and a hiccough. The plans and diagrams couldn't be found.

It was Homer and Freddy (still dressed as Indians, of course) who found the little wooden keg near the corner. They smelled it. They tasted it. Freddy shouted, "I know — it's cough syrup!"

"*And Elixir Compound!*" added Homer. "Dulcey dug it up! This is where Ezekiel buried it! And this is where the Homestead stood!"

That was it! And it didn't take the worthy tenants long to count their way home.

Old Doctor Pelly diagnosed Dulcey's trouble as "an overdose of Cough Syrup and Elixir of Life Compound, aged over a hundred years in a wooden keg." Dulcey was up and about the business of installing street signs late the next day.

One Hundred and Fifty Years of Centerburg Progress Week came to a close with peace and prosperity. Time and progress move ahead. The Ezekiel Enders Homestead moved back to take the place of the one hundred and first house too. You see, the worthy tenants, though up and coming, aren't taking any chances.

Meanwhile the whole nation is singing:

> Forty-two pounds of edible fungus
> In the wilderness a-growin'
> Saved the settlers from starvation,
> Helped the founding of the nation.
> Forty-two pounds of edible fungus
> In the wilderness a-growin'.'